Up Campus, Down Campus

THE **ADVENTURES** OF ANIRBAN ROY IN **JNU**

AVIJIT GHOSH

SPEAKING
TIGER

SPEAKING TIGER PUBLISHING PVT. LTD
4381/4, Ansari Road, Daryaganj
New Delhi 110002

First published in paperback by Speaking Tiger 2016

ISBN: 978-93-86050-55-7
eISBN: 978-93-86050-53-3

10 9 8 7 6 5 4 3 2 1

The moral right of the author has been asserted.

Typeset in Adobe Garamond Pro by SÜRYA, New Delhi
Printed at Manipal Technologies Ltd., Manipal

Avijit Ghosh works as a senior editor for *The Times of India* in New Delhi. Born in Agartala, he grew up in the small towns of Arrah and Ranchi. He graduated in history from St Xavier's College, Ranchi and earned his Master's and MPhil degrees from JNU, New Delhi.

A journalist for more than twenty-five years, he has written extensively on Hindi cinema and sports. He has also briefly been a film critic for *The Telegraph* and *The Times of India*. His previous works include *Bandicoots in the Moonlight*, a bildungsroman set in 1970s small-town Bihar, and *Cinema Bhojpuri*, which won the Special Mention for Best Writing on Cinema in the 2010 National Film Awards. His third book, *40 Retakes: Bollywood Classics You May Have Missed*, revisits a bunch of movies that have fallen through the cracks of our memory.

Avijit is addicted to films, music, football and cricket—not necessarily in that order. He tweets intermittently from the handle @cinemawaleghosh and eagerly awaits your detailed feedback at avijitghosh65@rediffmail.com

To JNU
For everything

Contents

Author's Note and Acknowledgements

Sometime in the 1980s, let us not talk about the year, I arrived with two friends in New Delhi after a tortuous 32-hour train journey. We were surrounded, almost harangued, by a bunch of taxi-drivers as we stepped out of the station. Most of them asked for 100 rupees for the long ride to JNU. We had been told back home to quote half of what they asked for. We did. It was a long negotiation. But finally, and I recall this with some pride, we paid a total of 50 rupees, maybe a few bucks more. For the next six years—with an involuntary gap in between—the campus became my home for at least 350 days a year. Slowly but surely, JNU reordered me.

This novel takes its emotional core from what I saw and lived through during those days. Like Anirban Roy, the protagonist of this novel, I came to JNU to prepare for the civil services. But Anirban is not me. Barring professors and other well-known individuals who have been named in the book, all characters are fictional. At places, I have taken the creative licence to align the narrative with contemporary political happenings. However, much of the physical description of the campus and the city is real. It is possible that other students, who were there at the same time, may argue that what they saw and experienced was entirely different. They are right, too. Truth, as Kurosawa showed us in *Rashomon*, isn't just what we see but also what we want to see.

Up Campus, Down Campus has been in the making and unmaking for the past three and half years. I started writing it in February 2013 when Devesh Kapur, who heads the Centre for the Advanced Study of India (CASI) in the University of Pennsylvania, generously offered me a two-month scholarship. Most of the first draft was hammered out during evenings at the iconic Penn Bookstore which was merely a curve ball throw from the hostel. Finishing the remainder of the book took me more than two years. Finding a publisher took a long time, too. It was a new and unsettling experience for me. A couple of publishers who rejected the manuscript told me that nobody is interested in reading about the JNU of the 1980s. This kept happening through the fall of 2015.

I am thankful to Ravi Singh of Speaking Tiger for showing unshakeable faith in the book much before JNU became a national talking point earlier this year. I sincerely thank Paromita Mohanchandra for editing the manuscript with care and empathy.

I take this opportunity to record my gratitude to my mentors: the late Bipan Chandra, Mridula and Aditya Mukherjee, K. Jagannadha Rao, Chandan Mitra, A.K. Bhattacharya, Devesh Kapur and Sidharth Bhatia. Also, my appreciation of friends and colleagues: D. Shyam

Babu, Chandrabhan Prasad, Susmita Dasgupta, Neeraj Singh, Sushil Aaron, Deepika Sahu, Anuradha Raman, Vinay Pandey, Nirmal Sharma, Malini Sen, Tirna Ray, Ronojoy Sen, Gautam Siddharth, Alok Sinha, Namrata Joshi, Jaideep Varma, Samita Bhatia, Ghazala Wahab, Pradeep Thakur, Syed Saud Akhtar, Sanjeev Singh, Asha Ramachandran, Renu Pachauri, Devlin Roy, Amit Lal, Bhaskar Pant, Dhananjay Mahapatra, Garima Pachauri, Sameer Arshad, Fozia Yasin, Monobina Gupta, Manoj Mitta, C.P. Surendran, Aarti Tikkoo Singh, Novy Kapadia, Rakesh Batabyal, Shishir Prashant, Vijay Lokpalli, Renuka Bisht, Sanjiv Shankaran, Diwakar, Ranjan Roy, Shankar Raghuraman, Subodh Verma, Atul Thakur, Surojit Gupta, Sidharth, Debashish Roy, Kim Arora, Juliana Di Giustini, Tanya and Art Carey, Alan Atchison, Anil Grover, Kaushik Ray, Debashish Roy, Rochan Pant, Kalyan Ghosh, Prita Maitra, Ronojoy Sen, Georgette Chryssanthakopoulos and Anit Mukherjee.

Some debts cannot be repaid. I can only express my eternal gratitude to my mother Anjali, my sister Bani and my Jamai babu, and my wife Rachna for everything they have done for me. Abhishek and Diya, without your active involvement this book might have been finished much earlier.

While writing this novel, I spoke to several friends from JNU. My regards to them for their 'ears and views'. They know who they are. Two books, *JNU: The Years* (edited by Kanjiv Lochan) and *JNU, The Making of a University* by Rakesh Batabyal, acted as occasional consultants. The novel also includes a few lines from two poems, one of them written by the great Turkish poet Nazim Hikmet, the other penned by Ernest Dowson. Both are long gone. But as this novel shows, their works continue to be remembered, appreciated and quoted. I had first read about Dowson in a popular column written by the multi-talented Khushwant Singh. For some reason, I never forgot the poem.

They say JNU is all about Marx
That's not entirely true
Ask any of the small-town boys who went there
Marx was the means
Freud, especially his sex thing, was the end…

1

First impressions

EVERY UNIVERSITY CAMPUS, like a song, has its own cadence. Anyone who steps inside must discover its secret rhythm. The lucky ones find something more than a home. Others just meander through a bunch of semesters meaninglessly and leave without memories much like a careless day-tripper.

But locating the pulse of a campus can take an awful lot of tact and time. It can be terribly tedious too, especially if you are fresh from the dustbowls of Inner India, without any degree in the nuanced art of listening and you arrive in an alternative planet called JNU, the famed Jawaharlal Nehru University.

The truth is that a new place, far away from family, can be unusually disorienting. The hours and the days don't move with the easy rhythm and certitude of a clock, or, a calendar. They are a goulash of chaotic moments which jump at you and vanish in equal haste.

It's equally true that there's no single, complete and definitive story of any campus; its social life and secret history, in this case, also its contagious politics. There are many JNUs and it depends on which one you went to. It is like a story with many versions: everybody has a version of his or her own.

And this is Anirban's version of his first day in the campus:

'When I slowly pushed the door open and stepped into my hostel room, I saw a young man and a younger woman spring apart, as if they had been electrocuted. I cannot say for sure what they were doing, but the girl seemed to be shellshocked. When the dude looked at me—just picture the moment and take a guess—he seemed to be holding two imaginary cricket balls in his hands.'

Of course, Anirban should have knocked on the door. But back home in Bihar where he had grown up, such manners were often confused for pansy behaviour. If you are up to something, why don't you bolt the fuckin' door? In any case, a girl was the last thing he was expecting inside a boys' hostel on his first day in the campus.

The girl's colour, Anirban observed, was like carrot blended in cream. She was remarkably tall, with a clever nose that defined her face. And her body was premium real estate. Clearly, she was a foreign student.

'Who are you?' the guy's voice was soft even though the bulge in his boxer shorts wasn't.

'I am Anirban Roy, your new roommate,' he replied, rather embarrassed at the interruption now.

'Oh,' the guy sighed in a way that implied resignation. 'I am Ravi Bhatia. As you must have found out, I am your roommate as well.' He flashed a half smile.

The girl, by then, had jumped out of the bed. Rather

boldly, she put her hands inside her red T-shirt that clearly had seen better days, to adjust a bra strap, which seemed to have been displaced from its preferred position. She didn't smile at Anirban or wish him hello.

'You have learnt nothing from what I taught you last night,' Bhatia was addressing her in Hindi.

He was ribbing, not rebuking, her.

The girl, who was definitely taller than both Bhatia and Anirban, suddenly folded her hands like an Indian Airlines air-hostess. 'JNU *mein aapka swaagat hai, manyavar,*' she said. Anirban smiled—not because she spoke in Hindi but because she had said '*manyavar*', a word probably last used in a conversation in the eleventh century CE. Only a foreigner who had learnt the word from a book would be using it. But Bhatia was triumphant. He patted her cheek. And Anirban couldn't help thinking that perhaps he might have employed a more intimate way of expressing his approval but for his roommate's unexpected presence.

Pleased at the welcome, Anirban too, replied in all seriousness, '*Dhanyawaad. Aapse mil kar bahut khushi huyee.*' She smiled for the first time. '*Mera naam* Svetlana Pashkova *hai. Main* USSR *se aayee hoon,*' she said.

Her manner of speaking reminded Anirban of the Russian heroine in Raj Kapoor's mega box-office turkey, *Mera Naam Joker.* Svetlana probably wanted to prolong the conversation but Bhatia cut her short. 'I will see you in the evening,' he said. She seemed sore at being stopped midway but decided against saying anything. She adjusted her bra strap again, opened the back door, flashed a quick sideways glance and slipped away.

2

The back-door policy

WITHIN A FEW days, Anirban found out that whenever he disclosed his room number to anybody in the hostel, the chap would become unusually friendly. He would try to make Anirban feel comfortable, offer help and generally try to please him. It was as if Anirban had a gate pass to some secret paradise they all wanted to visit.

On his fifth night in the campus, Anirban was wondering if his right hand could be used for some exercise, when he heard gentle, almost embarrassed knocking on the back door. Dressed only in his zebra-striped undies that one of his weirdo friends had gifted him on his nineteenth birthday back home, Anirban opened the door thinking it was Bhatia. Instead it was a senior he had been introduced to at lunch—who had generously offered him a 501 beedi after a rather unappetising lunch of kadhi-chawal.

'Can we just pass through?' he said softly. For a split second, Anirban deliberated on why he was addressing himself in the first person plural—and then he saw the answer emerge from the shadows: a dusky girl in dark blue jeans, with three bold and beautiful words printed in red on her white T-shirt, *Small is Beautiful.*

Anirban stared at her for a second and thought, *What a liar*! But before he could say, 'Sure. Cool. But please let me change into something decent first,' they had already breezed past him.

In JNU, like most universities, girls were not allowed into the men's hostels. But the liberal-minded architects of the building probably hadn't factored that in. For some reason, one side of the Periyar hostel was unprotected by a boundary wall. Anybody could easily slip into the hostel through one of the rooms on the ground floor, without attracting the attention of the guards.

But some rooms were inhabited by meanies who out of sheer spite refused to convert them into corridors for lovers. There were others, engrossed in serious studying for the civil services, who preferred not to be disturbed. They knew such lovers were creatures of habit, and if you opened the door once, you would have to repeat the act time and again.

Then there were the Ganga dhaba types, who were seldom available in their room before 1 a.m. Simply put, only about half a dozen rooms were available for entering or exiting the hostel surreptitiously, bypassing the guard at the front gate—and it made sense, especially if you had a girlfriend, to be pally with one of the co-owners of those rooms.

You never knew when you would need a favour.

Another strange thing happened the same night.

Anirban was about to sit down with the photostat copy of an old article from the *Scientific American*, a mandatory read for next day's Ancient Society class, when he heard a knock on the front door.

He thought it was certainly roomie Bhatia this time, but was surprised again to find a group of four students outside. One of them, who looked slightly familiar, smiled at him in a rather meaningful way that Anirban couldn't decode. Then the penny dropped: he was one of his classmates who had been introducing himself to every other student in class with a fake sincerity that reminded him of candidates contesting municipal elections back home.

'Hi, it's me, Joseph. You recognize me right? We met at the department today,' he said. Anirban nodded his head in agreement but without enthusiasm.

But for the guys, this was encouragement enough. One of them piped up with a smile. 'Can we speak with you for a few minutes? By the way I am P.M.S. Shankar, the SFI general secretary in JNU,' he said.

Shankar was neither wearing spectacles nor was he bearded. He wasn't dressed in a crumpled kurta, unwashed jeans and hawai chappals either. And he didn't have a half-smoked Charminar in hand. In fact, he was nothing like the stereotypical Commie that Anirban had conjured in his head watching Mrinal Sen movies. Shankar was neatly dressed in a blue shirt folded up to his elbows and grey trousers. The third male in the group had Fidel Castro written all over his beard. He was the strong and silent type.

The lone girl, smelling faintly of coconut oil and

Communism, bared her teeth. 'I am Geetha Kasturi,' she said and slipped back into the book she had brought along.

'Geetha is working on her doctorate on saints and vagabonds in thirteenth-century Rajasthan. It is the history of mentalities, you know.' It was Joseph again.

Anirban felt like saying something on the choice of her subject. But he couldn't come up with anything funny without being really rude.

He immediately banished the mischievous thought the moment she offered her hand. It was the first time Anirban had shaken hands with a girl after midnight. In fact, he recalled later, it was the first time he had ever shaken hands with a member of the female species.

'What's it you wanted to discuss?' he asked Shankar, who by now was sitting in one of the two chairs in the room. Chit-chat followed. They asked Anirban if he enjoyed the lectures, whether the mess food was okay and if it was a problem that the running water stopped exactly at 9 a.m. Anirban guessed, rather correctly, it was their way of putting him at ease.

One of them complimented him for the black-and-white poster of a pensive Che Guevara on the wall and was disappointed to find out that it actually belonged to one of the previous occupants.

'Imagine leaving behind such a beautiful poster!' Geetha exclaimed. Judging by her tone, the guy had apparently committed a crime worthy of the Gulag.

The intruders, however, were pleased to know that Anirban had been a member of the Left cultural troupe,

IPTA, back home in Ranchi and had acted in a few revolutionary plays for a coalminers' union in the heart of the Chhotanagpur plateau.

Anirban couldn't get himself to confess that his association was purely due to the fact that the director's generously breasted daughter, who was his college-mate, was the troupe's make-up artiste and therefore, always travelled with them. In the best tradition of small-town love stories in the 1980s, they hadn't even exchanged a hello.

And then they came to the grand topic of the evening. 'Has anybody offered you the membership of a political party?' Joseph asked.

'I have been here for just five days. Isn't that too early?' Anirban couldn't help asking.

Joseph and the rest of the gang laughed. Geetha almost rolled over with laughter on the bed and a vivid stream of pornographic moments ran through Anirban's sex-starved mind. 'No, actually we are running late, very late,' Joseph said.

All laughed again as if sharing an inside joke.

'Well, we want you to join the SFI,' Shankar was direct. His tone was gentle but it had the smell of *Godfather*—an offer you couldn't and shouldn't refuse.

'You just have to fill up a form. The membership charge is 25 paisa,' Shankar completed the offer. Anirban stopped himself from muttering, 'I don't carry that kind of cash.'

Seriously, it sounded like one of those great winter sale offers that were always too good to be true. And only after reading the fine print did one realize what one was getting into.

'25 paisa? Only?' Anirban wondered aloud if he had heard it right.

'Yes, it is just 25 paisa. And you don't have to bother. I will pay up,' Joseph said.

Who says a super bargain offer cannot be bettered?

As Anirban sat on the bed pondering over the offer, a couple of conversations with friends in Ranchi scurried through his mind.

'Why are you going to JNU?

'To prepare for the IAS. Isn't that obvious?'

'But don't you know that Delhi University is better for that?'

'I know. But unlike in DU, every student immediately gets a hostel seat in JNU. Everything is subsidized. That's important for me.'

'But the place is infested with Laal Jholawalas. They will turn you into a Commie and that will be the end of your civil services dream. And much like Alice in Wonderland, you will find yourself in a rabbit hole that won't be easy to get out of. Keep that in mind.'

'I will.'

'Best of luck.'

After a pause that seemed like an eternity, he finally said, 'Look can we do this some other day? I want to think it over.'

There was an embarrassed silence—much like if a bride were to fart in a wedding mandap. It was obvious that the gang of four had been confident of clinching the deal. Clearly, Anirban dragging his feet was a surprise, if not a shock, to them.

'But yaar, this is very simple. You know the Left all over the world is fighting US imperialism. If you sign up with us, it means you stand firmly behind those who are fighting for a better world,' Joseph said.

There was both a dash of desperation and a hint of consternation in his voice, which generally happens when you try to patronize somebody.

Joseph seemed to have promised his leaders that the boy was in his bag. Obviously, that wasn't the case. Now, he was going to lose a few brownie points with them.

'I know,' Anirban said, softly but firmly, 'but I just need some time to think it over. You know it is a big decision.'

'In JNU, the SFI is generally voted to power in the university elections. The NSUI (National Students Union of India) and the ABVP (Akhil Bharatiya Vidyarthi Parishad), exist only in name. That's why there's no eve teasing, no ragging in the campus. Did anyone bother you in the campus?'

'No,' Anirban quietly shook his head. But he also asked himself if JNU was the only place in the country where the Commies controlled a students' union. And if that wasn't the case, why the SFI couldn't stop violence and ragging in the colleges and universities of Bengal and Kerala where it also enjoyed power?

Seeing the newcomer was hesitant, Shankar patted him on the shoulder. 'Take your time, man. There's no hurry. Joseph will stay in touch with you.' He then gestured to the third guy in the group, who hadn't uttered a word yet, to get up.

Looking closely at him, Anirban realized that the Castro-like beard could have been a ploy to hide prominent portions of his pockmarked face. Geetha, who had been reading a book of poetry all along, also got up. 'Nice meeting you,' she said and shook his hands warmly again. It appeared as if she had been brought only to shake hands with the newcomer.

The joke went, Anirban learnt later, that small-town boys from Bihar and Uttar Pradesh didn't wash their hands for days after shaking hands with a girl. Well, that was an exaggeration. But the truth was that the prospect of meeting girls—'*Kaisi bhi, koi bhi*'—was always one of the big lures of joining student's politics in the campus.

'What are you reading?' Anirban asked.

'Oh, it is just a book of poems,' she said casually, as if to suggest, *this is way above your league.*

'Is it by Nazim Hikmet, the Turkish poet?' Anirban asked, having read the name on the cover.

Suddenly she was looking at him with a fresh pair of respectful eyes. Anirban hoped she would shake his hand a third time. He had once borrowed a collection of poetry from a theatre director while travelling for a play staged in Dhanbad. He remembered reading a poem by Hikmet over and over again during that bus journey. A couple of lines had stuck with him.

He recited:

I love you
like dipping bread in salt and eating
like waking up at night with high fever

and drinking water with the tap in my mouth
like unwrapping the heavy box from the postman
with no clue what it is
fluttering, happy, doubtful…

Everybody seemed impressed. Shankar's eyes seemed to be suggesting. 'Hey, we came looking for a cadre. But this guy could be more.'

Geetha just said, 'Oh, that's a lovely poem. I hope you are coming for the students' GBM at the auditorium at 9 o'clock tomorrow. Catch you there.' She smiled again.

Immediately after they had left, it struck Anirban that he did not know what GBM stood for.

He had barely sat down for 10 minutes when there was another knock at the front door. This time it was indeed Bhatia, smelling of alcohol, nicotine and Svetlana. 'Yaar,' he pleaded, 'I know you are studying seriously. But can you take a break for 30 minutes? It is very important.' He even slipped a five-rupee note into his palm. 'Just have some bun-omelette and nimboo-pani. It's JNU's national food and drink,' he joked.

And then to make matters crystal clear, he whispered, 'She is waiting at the back door.'

'Take your money back. You don't need to bribe me. I will be back in exactly 30 minutes,' Anirban said.

'*Yaar, bura to nahin maan gaya tu*, hope you haven't taken it too badly,' he said, without meaning a word of it. When he saw that Anirban hadn't, he immediately got down to being himself. 'Don't be punctual like the British, yaar. Five to ten minutes extra wouldn't harm any of us,' he winked.

Anirban walked quietly to the Nilgiri dhaba, ordered a glass of nimboo-pani, and sat down on a stone bench cursing Bhatia and hoping he suffered from premature ejaculation. He was trying to locate Venus in the night sky when he heard a female voice enquire, 'What are you doing here so late at night? I thought you were trying to shake us off because you wanted to study.'

Anirban turned around. It was Ms Kasturi. She was holding a small thermos flask in her hand. Anirban pretended to look at the flask while he ogled at the bumps on her chest for a second or so. Before he could say anything, she said, 'I came to buy some coffee for my roommate. She is preparing for the civil services. Aren't you interested in the IAS exams?'

Is that a trick question? Anirban wondered. He had been forewarned that JNU was perhaps the only place in India where preparing for the civil services was a clandestine activity of the lowlife. The teachers didn't want it. But more than that, in the land where deriding the system and positioning oneself as a rebel and a radical was the quintessence of campus cool, it was totally uncool to be hankering after the loaves and fishes of power. Anirban didn't know if she was sussing him out or the query was as innocent as the absent top button on her shirt. He mumbled something that sounded like a mix of 'maybe, I don't know.'

'You don't have to say it, if you don't want to,' Geetha said as if hurt by his unwillingness to come clean.

By now, Mahavir, the dhabawala, had filled up the flask.

'See you later,' she said and disappeared into the dark. It was much after she had left that Anirban realized that clouds had suddenly thrown a dark bedspread over the sky and he wouldn't be able to locate Venus. And he also realized that he had an erection.

3

Clueless in the campus

THE NEXT DAY, Anirban rolled out of bed for an early morning walk. Normally, his mother had to shout and shake him before he even stirred. Here he was up and about early, hoping to get a physical sense of the place.

It was late July but the monsoon had bypassed the metropolis. The sky was an infinite blue desert and the air was without humidity or hope. The birdsong, Anirban noted, had the clarity of a child's voice. At least there was something which reminded him of home. There were hardly any joggers in action. JNU didn't believe in early to bed and early to rise. And it didn't believe that health is wealth.

For the first time, Anirban stared intently at the hostel buildings lining up in this great educational estate. Distinct and dignified—the campus indeed was some place special in New Delhi. It was unlike anything he had seen since he arrived here in a taxi from the railway station.

JNU had fashioned style out of austerity. The burnt-red-brick buildings had an easy harmony of shape and colour.

Their symmetry created a sense of uniformity and order. The cemented sidewalks were lined up with a variety of trees that would delight any blue-blooded botanist. And the expansive tarred roads had the smoothness of cold-creamed cheeks. Cars and buses would probably have whizzed about on them but the speed-breakers, thoughtfully put up every 50 yards or so, demolished their hopes.

If the roads were orderly, the walls were chaotic. Looking at the graffiti, one could easily confuse Nicaragua as a South Asian neighbour and Cuba as another state of the Indian republic.

When the Leftist Nicaraguan president Daniel Ortega came to JNU, Anirban was told, the campus Commies got a collective O. Posters of praise, pamphlets resembling hosannas and banners lauding the new Left hero had colonized the campus like pimples on an adolescent face. Even Banbhatta, the court poet of the ancient Kannauj king Harshavardhan, would have found it impossible to improve on then.

JNU was physically defined not by its walls but by its rocks. The university was built on the Aravali ridge and giant boulders were everywhere. Those in the stone quarry business would have moaned at the colossal wastage of such a precious national resource. With no rough edges, the smooth rocks provided the best, and often the most intimate, benches on the campus. They were not just part of the campus landscape but also part of its personality, its existential core.

For fear of getting late, and worse, getting lost, Anirban

returned to the room within an hour. Water, or the lack of it, seemed to be taken for granted by the students. Like underclass colonies, the hostel got only a limited supply every day. The taps would burst to life around 7 a.m. and run dry by 9. Students would rush to complete their ablutions in those two hours. A difference of 30 seconds could push you back in the queue. The scene was repeated in the evening. But the rationed supply forced discipline among the hostellers, who queued up like inmates of a minimum security prison for the essentials.

Thankfully, the queues hadn't formed yet. After his late night exertions, Bhatia was still lost in sleep. Anirban hurried through the 3 Ss—shit, shave and shower—and quickly buried a wriggly fried egg with a half-burnt toast. He rapidly scanned *The Hindu*, the preferred newspaper of long-term civil services aspirants, picked up his notebook, stuffed it in his jhola, quietly shut the door and set out to attend his lecture. At least, he wanted to look the part.

His eyes spotted a hand-written message pasted on the door of Room No. 22: *Love is a kind of cancer with only one cure: chemotherapy of marriage. It kills the damn virus. It kills you too.*

JNU was sliced into two halves. The School of Languages (SL) and the School of International Studies (SIS) were part of the Old or Down Campus. The main library building and the School of Social Sciences (SSS) building, which housed the history department, were located in the New or Up Campus. Students commuted between the two campuses, separated by a couple of kilometres, on DTC buses every day. The old campus was gradually shifting to the new.

Anirban walked past the Kaveri hostel and the residences of Bipan Chandra and Yogendra Singh, the two dons of history and sociology. He crossed the road and walked past the trees and the bushes on the narrow trail towards the history centre.

He was about to enter the SSS building when he saw Robi Roy waving out to him. Robi had been a senior in Ranchi. It was a relationship that had never crossed the insincere, 'Hello, how are you?' stage. Here he was effusive like a half-lost girlfriend. 'Great to see you, man!' he gushed, 'I was told you would be joining us this year. But it had completely slipped my mind.'

Then he was all brass tacks, 'See, there's a GBM today. The SFI rules JNU because it is very powerful in the School of Social Sciences. You know what the SFI is, right? The student's wing of CPM, the Communist party that is fucking Bengal dry. We will have the student's union election in a few months. In this GBM, the SFI party students will flaunt what they have achieved in the past one year. That would be a pile of bullshit. The truth is they have done nothing. So the entire GBM is an eyewash. We must expose them. I know you have just arrived here a few days back. But I want you to be an important member of our party.'

'What party?' Anirban asked.

'The FTs, the Free Thinkers,' he said, with a hint of pride.

Just then Robi seemed to have spotted another newcomer. Rushing towards him, he shouted back, 'Meet me at the Sutlej hostel at 10 tonight. The room number is 142.' And he was gone. The thought that immediately swept across Anirban's mind was: *What has this place done to him? He was such a different guy in Ranchi!*

And then he remembered that he had again forgotten to ask what GBM meant.

Moments after Robi left, Joseph emerged from nowhere. 'How do you know Robi?' he asked.

'We went to the same college.'

'Is he a close friend?'

'No, we just know each other.'

'Was he asking you to join the Free Thinkers?'

'No,' Anirban lied.

'Good. Have you decided to join us?'

'No,' Anirban said. He wasn't lying now.

'That's okay. Take your time. The GBM is at the SSS auditorium on the ground floor. Come and see how we conduct our student meetings democratically. That's the SFI style,' he said.

'Would you please explain what GBM stands for?' Anirban finally managed to ask.

'General Body Meeting.'

Anirban walked into the hall rather gingerly. He wanted to settle down in an inconspicuous corner, where he could be mistaken for the furniture. That's when he heard someone drawl, 'Come here. Come to me, baby.'

Who talks like that in an Indian university? Anirban thought, and looked around only to find a girl waving at him.

She was dressed in a blue skirt that seemed to have had no contact with soap and a black sleeveless T-shirt parading her wildly bushy armpits. And her hairstyle was a serious copyright violation of Sai Baba's signature.

Is this ragging time? Anirban asked himself. But Ms Sai Baba was alone and certainly didn't look the ragging type. Sitting on the stairs that led to the hall's upper floor, she looked more like a hippie: anorexic and wrecked. As Anirban walked up to her, quivering and quizzical, he saw that her legs were wide apart, as if anticipating coitus. And she was smiling at him. Was it derision or what, he just couldn't figure out.

'Are you from Bihar?' she asked him.

Anirban was finally convinced it must be derision.

'Yes. Why? Do I smell of Bihar?' he asked, taking care not to reveal his irritation.

Sensing his discomfort, she grasped his hands, pulled him forward and clasped him between her legs. When he was barely 11, Anirban had been fondled by a friend's elder sister. And during a hiking trip some years later, he had been offered a lift by a truck driver who had asked him if he would mind playing with his 'auzaar' while his college mates played antakshari in the back. It was obvious he didn't mean the tools in the gear box.

This was equally unexpected.

'*Mujhe jaane dijiye.* Let me go,' Anirban bleated like a lamb. Thank God, there was nobody in the vicinity.

'Not before you answer a few questions,' she said. 'My first question is: have you read Antonio Gramsci?'

'No,' he stumbled.

Sai Baby/Senior Senorita paused before shooting her second question. 'Have you ever kissed a girl?'

Anirban blushed.

She looked deep into his eyes, smiled cryptically and set him free. Then she got up, swept up her skirt and walked out of the hall.

What was that all about? Anirban wondered.

Too shaken to attend the GBM, he quietly slipped out of the auditorium.

He scurried to the library canteen, asked for black coffee and found himself a quiet place among the rocks. Anirban knew he was in another planet—a place unlike anything he had seen or imagined before, a place with an alternate set of norms. Or, maybe, it was just his luck that he had run into a few bizarre specimens, a visible minority anywhere. Surely he needed to find his own kind, and fast. *But equally importantly*, he thought, *I must keep a diary of such weird events and every other impression that the campus makes on me. Who knows, they could be life lessons.*

And also, because people should know how and why I went mad, he told himself.

4

The initiation

IT WAS AROUND 10.30 p.m. when Anirban reached Robi's hostel room where an anti-social zero power bulb was spreading more darkness than light. The room was just 10 feet by 10 feet in size. But it seemed endless, like an absurd play in a weird, wonderful way. Distances had been blurred by the bashful blue light and the haze of smoke. And Anirban's olfactory organs encountered a smell he had first chanced upon one summer evening around a group of sadhus on the ghats of Benaras. *I could get high or get lung cancer or both by just standing here for 15 minutes*, he thought.

Anirban saw two shadowy figures sitting with their backs to the wall. They looked totally some place else. The door leading to the balcony was ajar. And he could hear a strange grunting noise coming from that side. He couldn't figure out what was happening out there. It was either someone having sex or getting beaten up. Or getting beaten up while having sex.

Anirban didn't know either of the two blokes and

was rather hesitant to introduce himself to two spaced-out guys.

He was about to walk away when someone tapped him on his shoulder. 'When did you come?' It was Robi. The cologne he had showered himself with was powerful enough to make its presence felt even in that mushroom cloud of marijuana.

'Just a few seconds ago,' Anirban mumbled.

'Let me introduce you to everyone then,' Robi was playing the generous host. 'This is Jack. Jack Tiwary. He was the Free Thinkers' presidential candidate last year. And that is Manoj Mahapatra. If you have any conceptual problem in sociology, feel free to talk to him. He is a master of structuralism.'

Anirban murmured a reverential hello. He could see hands raised in slow motion in acknowledgement, although he didn't hear any accompanying sound to support the gestures.

'Jack, this is Anirban. You remember, I was talking to you about him? He is an old friend back from St Xavier's, Ranchi. We need guys like him if we want to challenge the Commies seriously in SSS.'

Jack leapt up faster than a Jeff Thomson bouncer.

'Let us go to the roof,' he said.

It was a request that sounded like an order. Anirban knew he was getting into a similar kind of situation that had got him entangled the night before. *The only difference is that unlike the SFI chaps, I know these guys*, he assured himself.

When you are in a new, strange place, at least in the first few weeks or months, you look for familiar hooks to hang on to. And in the process, you end up doing things that you may not do otherwise. Robi was Anirban's only anchor in JNU. That's why, even though going up to the roof did not appear to be a great idea, he obediently followed them out of the room.

Just as the three were about to step out, the balcony door opened. A guy in his undies stood wiping sweat off his hairy torso. 'This is my neighbour, Rohit Sangwan. We call him Rohit Jat, which sounds like one of those gangsters from Haryana, and makes him feel good about himself. He is working on his PhD in Russian poetry, with special focus on Pushkin. I have kept my bed in his balcony to create space for more people here. So he uses my balcony for his exercise,' Robi explained.

Rohit smiled but left in rather undue haste. It took some weeks for Anirban to figure out that being a bodybuilder was like being a leper in JNU. Flaunting body parts immediately plonked you at the bottom of the intellectual food chain.

There was an inverse snobbery about being unkempt and unmuscled, if not entirely scrawny. In fact, the casually messy look—untidy and uncombed—was actually a carefully cultivated appearance, a sort of image management in terms of what was the best marketable personality in the campus.

The rooftop was full of Free Thinkers. Everybody was dipping plastic cups into a pink bucket kept in a corner.

The bucket was filled with some kind of orange liquid with small apple chunks floating like debris in a sea. A couple of foxy chicks were also sipping the sweet shit and talking tutorials. They gave Jack the kind of looks which could be best described as half desirous and half self-denial.

In a few minutes, a fair and lovely girl emerged out of nowhere in a translucent top and dark jeans that were tight enough to suffocate any stray insect. Soon she was clinging to Jack as if he was the last raft of the sinking *Titanic*.

Jack introduced her to Anirban. 'This is Namita Chawla. She is one of our councillors in the School of International Studies. She won by a record margin last year. And Namita, this is Anirban, Robi's friend from Ranchi. He has just joined us.'

Anirban immediately wanted to say, 'Really? But when?' But something inside him again whispered that he shouldn't be asking too many questions at this point. Discretion, as they rightly say, is the better part of valour.

Anirban wasn't a political animal. So far, his own association with politics was limited to an unforgettable one-afternoon stand. He had voted four times in the 1977 Lok Sabha elections as a teenager: three times for the newbie Janata Party (because everybody was doing it) and once for the Congress (because the party's polling agent had given him Rs 5). All in the space of two hours. Simply put, he was a part of what was then called 'mass bogus voting', a rather popular phenomenon in north Indian politics till T.N. Seshan came and spoilt the party. Literally.

On the roof, Jack walked a few paces away from the

gathering and made himself invisible in a dark corner. Anirban followed him like a natural cadre follows a born leader. 'Tell me first what the SFI guys told you. Did they ask, what's your ideology?'

Anirban wasn't as much attracted to politics as to women and films. *This is going to be painful*, he thought. 'No, they were more direct. They just wanted me to join the SFI,' he said

'Okay,' Jack seemed to be warming up. 'Let me ask you then: what's your ideology?'

Ideology.

Anirban had been forewarned that the word would be hurled at him—both as flowers and stones. Like thousands before him, he had never encountered the word in a conversation before stepping into the campus.

Little did he know that in JNU, ideology was everywhere: in the mess, common room, dhabas, protest marches, seminars, classrooms, even commodes. Like an omnipotent virus, it was all over the campus.

Ideology was a catch-all word. Anything you couldn't explain by logic, you attributed to ideology. A conversation on ideology, as a veteran ideologue once told Anirban many months later in a confessional moment, was also the best foreplay in the campus.

But right now, Anirban had no answers. He made a quick mental note of looking up what it meant. 'I don't know,' he replied meekly, a little unsure if the answer would downgrade him in the eyes of Jack and Namita.

Jack smiled. And as Anirban realized later when he had

interacted more with him, it was not a smile of derision; rather, it was predatory. It was the smile that came when somebody invited him to play God. For many who fancied themselves as intellectuals in JNU, as Anirban was to find out, pontificating on politics was the ultimate rush, the stiffest hard-on.

'Let me first tell you a few basic things about the campus: Politics is the lifeblood of JNU. Only two things matter here: excellence in academics and the colour of your politics. The Congress-backed NSUI has only a marginal presence in the campus. Being a member of the NSUI means you have to kiss goodbye to being part of any meaningful social group. They are almost like pariahs. The ABVP doesn't even have a token presence here. They are worse than pariahs. That is quite remarkable, considering that both are such powerhouses in the Delhi University. For years, they have been trying to make inroads into JNU but without much success.

'Politics here is a caste system in itself. The SFI is the brahmin of JNU politics. With the All India Student's Federation (AISF), which is affiliated to the Communist Party of India (CPI), they share a now-on, now-off relationship like a couple in a Woody Allen movie. Then there's DRSO, the Delhi Radical Students' Organization, the radical Commies with more leaders than cadres.

'The campus politics is in harmony with the academia. JNU is an intellectual fortress of the Left. The university owes its existence to the Congress's dalliance with a section of the Communists in the 1960s. The university was set up as a barometer to measure the Left's temperature. As it happens with any cadre-based organization, the Commie academics have taken control of every sinew of the syllabus. Most prescribed articles and books point Leftward,' Jack was gushing like an uncontrollable river.

'I have seen that they hate everything about the US,' Anirban chipped in with his two-bit observation.

'You are right. For all these Commies, capitalism is evil, something worse than child abuse. For them, praising the US is like sleeping with your grandmother. Any US supporter is either 'a paid dog of the CIA' or 'a capitalist roader'.

'Nothing turns on a Commie more than a tirade against the US. If all the 'US Down Down' slogans shouted during student demonstrations in the past 10 years was put together on a sheet, it would have travelled all the way to Moscow and back.'

Anirban couldn't say whether he was high or not. But Jack's eyes were pretty red. And he was in no mood to stop.

'Now let me explain what we Free Thinkers stand for. We are not Leftists. But we respect Marx the philosopher, the social scientist. You know, he once said, "Doubt everything". Our touchstone is reason. We think, evaluate and judge everything on the basis of rationality. In the SFI, you don't think for yourself. The party decides everything for you. You are just a mindless cog in a monster wheel.

'Being in a Communist party is like being in a cult: without any personality or individuality. You don't have the right to criticize the gods out there—the Lenins and the Stalins. Do you know, they haven't criticized China even today for the 1962 aggression? They will promise you a revolution and a utopia where everyone is equal. But it will never happen.

'Do you know why? Because the concept is inherently flawed. Where is the dictatorship of the proletariat that Marx envisaged? Can you see it anywhere in the Soviet Union or in its satellites in Eastern Europe? What you see everywhere is the dictatorship of the party and its elites. If you are an important member of the Communist Party, you are the biggest social and political elite of all. But if you are not, you are doomed. Especially if you have a mind and you want to put it to use. Look what they did to a world-class writer like Alexander Solzhenitsyn. Given an opportunity, they will do the same in India.'

Anirban listened in awe. To him, Jack was Vivekanand, Churchill and Osho wrapped into one. For a moment, he imagined himself to be swapping places with Jack: lecturing newbies with a sexy arm candy like Namita in tow. But Jack wasn't done yet.

'Unlike the Marxists, we don't believe in Utopias. We are not in the business of selling lies. We, the Free Thinkers, just promise that we will never begin a debate with a conclusion and then work backwards. Here we start a debate and arrive at an honest conclusion. Everybody is heard and respected.'

Jack would have probably continued in the same vein for the next few months but was gently interrupted by Robi, who had arrived holding a paper cup dripping with rum punch. He whispered something in Jack's ear to which he replied, rather dismissively, '*Abhi nahin*, not now.' Robi whispered something again in his ears. This time Jack reluctantly said, '*Theek hai*, okay.' Robi immediately slunk away, leaving Anirban to face Jack's firing-squad sermon again.

'I have a lot of respect for the radical Left. Some of the best minds of their time left their colleges and the prospect of a great career to fight for the rights of ordinary people and carry out a revolution in the hinterland of Bihar. They were the real Leftists. These guys are caricatures of the Left. You know there are only two selfless relationships in the world: *Ma ka bacche ke prati aur Naxaliyon ka Mao ke prati*—a mother's bond with her child and a Naxalite's love for Mao. But these are *sarkari* Leftists. Forget radicalizing the students, they can't even radicalize the trade unions they control. Tell me, why is Bengal going down the drain under the Marxists?'

Despite being a Bengali by biology, Anirban had no idea that Bengal was going down the drain. Back home in Ranchi, he had spent most of his time ogling at girls, watching movies and discussing cricket (in that order) with friends who roughly followed the same lifestyle.

But the truth is that girls occupied Anirban's mindspace like nothing else. Everything else was a waste of time. They consumed his fantasies. Thinking about them and doing things to them in reveries was the lightning rod of his life. They powered and energized his being. But that was hardly anything unique. Every guy he knew was much like him. Each of them loved discussing the girls in class, dissecting their anatomies. And yet most of them were terribly tongue-tied and utterly polite to them in real life. They were all promiscuous virgins or almost-virgins. Promiscuous in their fantasies, virginal in real life.

His father constantly urged, and occasionally admonished, him to read the edit page of the highly revered *The Statesman*. But he found himself being attracted only to the sports pages.

Anirban remembered reading reports of Hindus being killed in Punjab, of Operation Bluestar, of the assassination of Prime Minister Indira Gandhi, the photographs of Sikhs slaughtered in Delhi. He also couldn't forget the faces of the two elderly Sikhs in the neighbourhood being lynched during the anti-Sikh riots in Ranchi.

He was also aware that a Jharkhand movement demanding a separate state for Adivasis was on. Every now and then, a Chhotanagpur bandh would bring the town to a standstill. During rallies, the sprawling Morabadi maidan near his home would be filled with Adivasis, who would come from the heart of the plateau, carrying bows and arrows. It was a thrilling and fearful sight—though like thousands of others, he wasn't exactly sure whether a new state would be good for outsiders like him.

The walls of Ranchi were filled with slogans—*Shoshak diku, Chhotanagpur chhodo* (Exploiter-outsiders, leave Chhotanagpur). Like thousands of others, Anirban too, wondered if he was a diku or not. Diku was the term given to 'outsiders' during the late-nineteenth-century Birsa

Munda rebellion against British authority. Somehow that term had returned to haunt the town. But those were the outer limits of his knowledge of contemporary national and regional politics.

'Tell me, why is Bengal going down the drain?' Jack asked him again. Anirban shook his head in a manner that suggested 'yes, no and maybe' all at the same time. He had learnt quickly that ambiguity was an effective protective shield in such situations of ignorance.

Whatever he meant, Jack took it as an answer that needed illustration. He grinned widely, letting out the beatific smile of a satisfied preacher and revealing his gutkha-stained teeth. Then he said something that took Anirban by surprise. 'I guess if I ask you what's your ideology you will say, "I don't know." Is that right?'

For once Anirban nodded with sincerity.

'In that case, you are a born Free Thinker,' he said with an unshakeable certitude. In his arms and silent all the while, Namita suddenly purred like an impatient cat. Taking the cue, Jack told him, 'Go and have some more drinks.'

Then he paused and said, 'We are leaving now but we will be back shortly.'

Anirban joined the larger group on the other side of the roof. It seemed a few other newcomers like him were also being initiated into the party by other seniors. He was not much of a drinker, but he hung around long enough to find out three things: that he could hold his fourth drink, that Jack was actually Jaikishen and that he did not keep his word of coming back soon.

5

Late night with Kimi Katkar

ANIRBAN HEARD AN obscene roar rise from the common room, located right above the mess, when he returned to the hostel. He decided to take a detour.

The common room was packed like a stadium in an Indo-Pak ODI game. All the sofas, even the space on the dusty carpet that every asthmatic student would have been mortally scared of, had been monopolized by the Biharis and the Oriyas. The Andhra guys were mostly standing at the back. Some of them were still holding bottles of gunpowder pickle in their hands that they generally brought to add some spice and taste to the food, which they considered too bland. This meant that they hadn't gone back to their rooms since dinner. It was nearly 12.30 a.m.

Some hostellers had pooled in money and hired a VCR. On seeing Anirban, one of the guys snuggled up to him. 'Arre yaar, we forgot to tell you about the show. Very sorry. But you haven't missed the best part. This movie will be over by 2.30. Only a few of us will be left by then. Then we will have a special show,' he winked.

Anirban tried hard to remember when he had met the guy but couldn't. Then it struck him that maybe he was one of the guys whom he had granted safe passage. For a moment Anirban felt like Humphrey Bogart in *Casablanca*. Like the Hollywood actor, he too, was helping lovers through, even at some personal risk. He liked the idea of lovers finding release in a country where pre-marital sex was regarded as a sin, if not a crime, in most regions.

And he understood what the guy had meant by winking at him. It meant they were going to show a b-f, the respectable abbreviation for a blue film.

Adventures of Tarzan, a B-grade Bollywood version of the famous jungle boy, was the centre of attraction right now. Apparently, the movie had one number, *Tarzan my Tarzan*, which was total paisa-vasool. Everybody was waiting for it as eagerly as farmers wait for the monsoon.

There wasn't much to amuse or entertain in a JNU common room. A carrom board with a missing striker and a table tennis table without the net was all that existed in the name of indoor sports. But the object of desire was a 21-inch Weston colour TV where Doordarshan reigned supreme.

The 9 p.m. news was like the late evening prayer you couldn't miss. Newsreaders Salma Sultan, J.B. Raman, Avinash Kaur Sareen, Minu, Geetanjali Aiyyar were like family friends who visited you every evening. Few watched the prime time serial. The bi-weekly *Chitrahaar* had its share of devotees though.

The common rooms were much more than avenues of

recreation. They were like mofussil single-screen theatres where boys could be boys and men could be men. The jokes were coarse, the laughter coarser. Sentences were incomplete without mentioning female private parts.

The common room turned into a greenhouse during summer. Often, as heat and sweat got the better of the impotent ceiling fan, guys would take off their shirts and whirl them around, hoping for a whiff of cool air. Their efforts would be futile because the air churned out was too hot and hostile for any relief.

Yet the heat failed to crush the enthusiasm of youth. Nothing matched the primordial thrill of the Indo-Pak ODI games. Till 1985, India had a fairly creditable record against Pakistan, especially on the big occasions. Already the world champion in 1983, India also claimed the Benson and Hedges Championship, a sort of alternative ODI World Cup played in Australia in 1985.

The same year, India had beaten Pakistan in another tournament in the not-so neutral venue of Sharjah. But that was the beginning of a drought for India against their bitter rivals.

These desert duels were watched passionately by immigrant workers from both countries in the stadium and generated as much mindless mania at home. The JNU common rooms became temples of hysteria where every umpiring error was furiously debated.

Some insisted there was a tinge of the communal in these games. There was a view that some students, especially those in the Arabic Studies department, wanted Pakistan to win, although they would never openly cheer for them. Others insisted that a subterranean anti-minority feeling was part of the anti-Pak sentiment among some students.

But that night everyone was united in anticipation. Some of them had already seen the movie and had already described in delicious detail what Ms Kimi Katkar did during the song. 'Last hai,' someone said. It was a phrase used to indicate the outer limit of extreme.

Then it happened. There they were—a desi Tarzan with his desi Jane—by the side of pouring waterfalls. Ms Katkar wore a red wraparound revealing her endless legs and a bikini bra of sorts, displaying enough space in between to place a chessboard over her bellybutton.

Long-haired and topless Tarzan was understandably even more underdressed. Only a small piece of cloth, the size of two decent-sized handkerchiefs, covered his unmentionables.

Tarzan My Tarzan was a seduction song, crooned by Alisha Chinoy, her voice on the far side of husky. It was clear within seconds that the love Ms Katkar sang about wasn't exactly the type Meena Kumari had immortalized in *Pakeezah*. Here was a heroine overcome by wanting, desperate to arouse her innocent lover to the pleasures of the mating game.

She bit him on his ears. She kissed him softly all over his hands. She positioned her legs in a manner that almost gave him a sight of her privates. She climbed on his back, rode over him in the water. And she jumped into a pool of water urging him to touch her '*phool sa bheega badan*'.

Even those vamps, shaking and shimmying their wares in low-lit nightclubs, were less upfront.

Gasps of wonderment and wolf-whistles of delight followed. As she wriggled and wiggled with an unbearable pleasure to every Bappi Lahiri beat, her body seemed to bend with desire, anticipating a million orgasms. This was simply the sexiest song they had ever seen.

That night, to a band of horny boys and men, Ms Katkar became the last word for lust, the poster girl of their fantasies. When the song ended, there was a collective boom: Once More! The track was a little long, five minutes and 25 seconds to be precise, but they saw it again and again and again. It was only after the number had been played a fourth time that the rewind button was given a rest.

Anirban wasn't in the mood for late night porn but the guy, who seemed to be the organizer, insisted he stayed back.

The show began around 2.40. The crowd by then had dwindled from 125 to 25. You could label them the most frustrated or the most committed.

The film's print wasn't in the best of health. But nothing mattered—not even that the actors spoke Swedish and that there were no sub-titles. Someone did remark, though, that the School of Languages should start a department in Scandinavian languages—and it certainly wasn't because he was a Bergman fan.

The length of the hero's member left everyone laughing in awkward awe after, possibly, a subconscious self-appraisal.

The conversations in the common room went like this:

'*Wahan kya kar raha hai ?*' *(*What is he doing down there?*)*

'*Main bhi wohi soch rahan hoon, maharaj.*' (Even I am thinking on the same lines, man.)

'*Are baap re, poora nigal jayegi kya?*' (Oh brother, will she swallow the whole damn thing?)

'*Ho sakta hai. Dekhiye mooh kitna kitna chauda hai.*' (Possible. See what a big mouth she has.)

When one of the guys got up to leave, there were wisecracks all round. '*Paanch ungliyon ki varjish karne jaa rahe ho, kya*? Are you going to exercise your five fingers or what?'

It was a shared joke, codified down the years in hostel culture.

'I think these guys use drugs. Otherwise it is not possible to perform like this. What do you say?' someone asked Anirban.

Speak for yourself, punk, is what Anirban wanted to say.

'Looks like it,' he replied aloud before killing any chance of a longer discussion with a hasty 'Good night.'

As he hit the sack, Anirban hoped to wander off to sleep. But the sights and sounds of the film's versatile female protagonist kept him awake for a long time. He also considered release. But the fact that Bhatia was sleeping just five feet away stopped him.

6

Lost in the campus

IT TOOK ANIRBAN more than a few weeks to realize that his class was filled with girls of astonishing but distraught beauty. He was like the street-kid standing in front of a toy shop. They looked so unattainable. They fascinated, scared and gave him an acute complex. There were 14 girls in his class. He was half in love with half of them.

There was Niharika, a frail, unblemished work of art who had Chicago University written all over her T-shirt and term papers. There was Sheba, dazed and confused. Her friend, Shumona, who always seemed elsewhere.

Vandana was avante-garde. She reminded Anirban of a line from the novel, *The Postman Always Rings Twice*—'Her lips stuck out in a way that made me want to mash them in for her.'

Neeta's jhola was always full of Marx and grass. But for the minor detail that he was dead, she would have lost her virginity only to Che, she once confessed in class. During orgasms, the joke went, instead of screaming *Oh my God*, she shouted, *Oh my Che, Oh my Che*.

Of course, there were a couple of 'bahenji' types too. Reeta was one, always talking Barabanki, the town she came from, and civil services.

Many of these girls had the polish of convent school. You could smell the urban cool in their accent, clothes and poise. Ethnic wear was hot and happening. Junk jewellery, especially earrings the size of a small mango, were excellent accessories for revolution. The anti-feminist chunni, though discarded by many, wasn't a total anachronism.

The boys, most of them from Bihar and Uttar Pradesh, were gaunt small-town rats desperately seeking something to cover the gaps in their flawed, incomplete selves. But slipping into baggy pants only made them appear more desperate. You could never tell, or maybe one could if you looked close enough, that they went to the same class. The two genders were separated by light-years.

Anirban realized the barometers of excellence were totally different from those in college back home. He had more cricket and film statistics in his head than most around. I mean how many remember that Sunil Gavaskar had acted in a Marathi film, *Svali Premachi* (Shadow of Love). In Ranchi, trivia like this had made him a local quiz champion. Here it mattered very little.

In his early teens Anirban had spent hours clutching his Bush Baron transistor by his side. He remembered names of the songwriters and composers of almost any Hindi film track that Vividh Bharati and Radio Ceylon played. Here they preferred the anti-establishment songs by Leftist cultural troupes, IPTA and Parcham, reeking of revolution and resistance.

He also remembered dozens of classical Urdu ghazals by heart. Mirza Ghalib, Mir Taqi Mir—he could quote them at an instant. But in the campus, Neruda, Paash and Dushyant Kumar were the unofficial poet laureates.

Anirban loved reading Hindi and Urdu literature, especially the short stories of Nirmal Verma, Mohan Rakesh, Saadat Hasan Manto and Rajinder Singh Bedi. He could engage with anybody on these masters of words and feelings. But here he felt inadequate. As Jack had told him, the only thing that mattered in JNU was accolades in academics and visibility in politics. Of course, you needed a few accessories too: cotton jholas that carelessly dangled from your shoulder and a pair of hawai chappals carved out of used car tyres to emphasize how successfully you had de-classed yourself.

The lectures were an eye-opener for Anirban. He had never come across teachers like these. So eloquent, so knowledgeable. So openly Left. Everything was wonderfully informal. You could call them by their first names. Some professors even invited students to their homes to discuss term papers. They treated students as grown-ups, if not equals. Asking questions wasn't 'acting smart' as his college lecturers believed back home. Probably it helped that there were only 22 students in the class.

Within a few lectures, Anirban had figured out that earning a post-graduate degree in modern history would be the most challenging project of his life. Going through the reading list for any term paper—an impressive but intimidating catalogue of published articles, research papers and books where the footnotes were often longer than the texts—he understood that the difference between what he had learnt back home and what he was being taught here was wider than he could ever hope to bridge. The syllabus was so different that he might have been studying some totally different subject so far. Anirban realized he had to read more pages in the next four months than he had done in three years of college.

Back home, he had been taught the history of dates and dynasties. One empire ended, another regime began. He had a sharp memory and enjoyed recreating in his mind's eye the battles of Haldighati, Panipat and Plassey.

In JNU, that history was pre-historic. Bunk.

Nobody spoke about R.C. Majumdar, Jadunath Sarkar, Stanley Lane-Poole and Vincent Smith—historians he had grown up with. They were obsolete. Bunk.

This was the history of ideas and concepts. Marxist ideas and concepts, to be precise. History was divided into too many schools: neo-colonial, nationalist, Marxist, subaltern and others. Broadly speaking, the Marxist school dominated the history department.

In the lecture room, Karl Marx wasn't just the reigning deity—he was Brahma, Vishnu and Mahesh rolled into one. Historians who had used Marxian tools to understand political and social shifts such as Eric Hobsbawm, Maurice Dobb, E.P. Thompson, Andre Gunder Frank, Fernand Braudel and Antonio Gramsci ('Aha, so that's what the weird girl in the auditorium wanted to know!') were deified.

Hegemony, modes of production, underdevelopment, class consciousness and dialectical materialism—words like these and thousands of others, teased and taunted him, much like a relentless bully in school. Anirban felt overpowered and flattened by the hordes of jargon. He had never felt so helpless in a classroom before.

It wasn't just the jargon; it was also the tyranny of ideology that irritated Anirban. There was little openness to non-Marxist ideas. Anybody who wasn't a Marxist was made to feel like an ignoramus yet to see the light, a slave of false consciousness.

Anirban found it hard to stomach the view that, both inside classrooms and outside, Gandhi was looked at as a sort of comprador bourgeois leader and not the Mahatma he had believed in all along. It was fashionable to be contemptuous about the Father of the Nation. 'If he wasn't there, the Communists would have created a workers' and peasants' revolution in India,' was a common enough view.

'There are two great tragedies in Indian history,' said a professor of intellectual history. 'The first is, Vivekanand coming under the spell of Ramakrishna Paramhans. The other is Nehru coming under the influence of Gandhi.' According to him, Nehru had great potential to be a revolutionary leader but lost his edge due to Gandhi. Same with Vivekanand and Paramhans.

What kind of a place have I landed up in where they have no respect for national icons? Where they respect Mao more than Gandhi? Anirban asked himself.

One afternoon, during a lecture on primitive society

that could have been in Greek for all he cared—and that too, in capital letters—Anirban started scanning the face of every student he could see. Most of them were listening attentively but he couldn't make out if they were doing it out of reverence or because they were engrossed in the lecture. Was he, then, the biggest duffer in the class?

'I want you to submit the tutorial by Friday,' he could hear the professor saying. 'And here's the reading list. Please distribute it among yourselves.'

As he sat in the department canteen, quietly sipping chai, a classmate he hadn't spoken to before walked up to him. 'Hello. My name is Sharad Rai. I saw you looking bored and distracted in the class.'

'I wasn't bored. I was confounded. Couldn't understand a damn thing. I am getting chewed up and spat out every day,' Anirban replied, rather peevishly.

'Where are you from?'

'Ranchi.'

'Okay. I can see your problem. What they teach us back there is so different from what they teach here. You need at least six months to get the hang of things. You must buy the dictionary of Marxism. It will make things easier for you.'

'Really?' He was surprised that a book like that even existed.

'Of course, it does. You can buy dictionaries of history, sociology and economics, if you want. You will get it at the bookshop in Kamal Complex. You must understand and internalize the social science jargon that the professors spew. That's the only way to get in control.'

'How do you know all this?' Anirban was pretty curious.

Sharad smiled, 'I come from south Bihar like you. Actually, I am from Jamshedpur. But I graduated in history from Delhi University. I have a friend who was here two years ago. He told me how the system really works and what you must do to impress these Commie professors. But I guess, you might have other questions in your mind too.'

'Like what?'

'Like do I want to work on my PhD for six years and become a middle-aged lecturer in a remote university? Or, should I use JNU as a cheap, transit guesthouse to clear the civil services?'

'Of course, I want to clear the civil services,' Anirban was excited. Finally, he had found someone who seemed to be on the same page.

'Well, in that case, you must do your post-graduation seriously. If you start preparing for civil services now, you will get terrible grades. And what if you fail to make it in the first attempt? Then it will be difficult for you to get admission for the MPhil programme. So my suggestion is: do your MA properly. Then clear the MPhil examination and get your hostel seat. After that, you can prepare seriously because there's very little MPhil class work,' Sharad said. He seemed to have everything planned to the last detail.

But Anirban wasn't sure. 'My father cannot support me that long. My family situation doesn't allow me to have a five-year plan.'

'Everything will change once you get into MPhil. You

can clear the UGC (the University Grants Commission) test. Then you will get Rs 800 every month as a scholarship. You won't have to ask for money from your parents. The important thing is that the scholarship is soon going to be raised to Rs 1,800 per month. Then you can live like a king.'

'What about you? Are you also preparing for the civil services?'

'Not at all,' he smiled. 'I want to spend my next five years reading all the books the professors don't ask you to read. I am seeking out all the renegade intellectuals—all those who were good enough to go to SOAS, or Chicago University but opted to stay back. I want to meet the washed out and the wasted. I want to attend every seminar, every political demonstration. I want to fuck every girl who wants to fuck me. I want to get drunk and hear Ramashankar Yadav 'Vidrohi' recite his poems.'

'Who is he?'

'He is a poet of the subaltern, the unrelenting rebel of the campus,' Sharad explained.

He then delivered his punch line, 'And I want to paint every wall with the slogan, *Free Nelson Mandela.*'

And Sharad was gone.

As he walked back to the hostel, Anirban kept looking at the JNU walls. Soon he realized that Sharad wouldn't have to work hard on at least one count. Half the walls in JNU were already covered with posters that bellowed *Free Nelson Mandela.*

7

A blind classmate

ANIRBAN WAS TRYING hard to decipher an article on the hunting-gathering age published in the *Scientific American*. If reading was anything like running uphill with a kilo of sand tied to each leg, this was it. For every fourth sentence, Anirban had to consult the dictionary of history. Which is why he took 45 minutes to fumble through an article of three pages. And even then, he couldn't make full sense of it. He felt that Sharad could help him. But he couldn't locate him in the 9 a.m. class the next day.

He found Sharad at the mess in the afternoon. 'I don't attend Ancient Society lectures. They bore me to death. In any case, I slept late at night. We watched Tarkovsky's *Stalker* at the Film Club last night. What a movie, yaar,' Sharad told him.

The Film Club was an extension of JNU's Marxist face. You only saw films made by Russian, Polish or Hungarian filmmakers. Even Bergman was too bourgeois for those who ran the show. The Commies in JNU believed in controlling every cultural forum. That, by the way, also included the mountaineering club.

Sharad seemed to be in the mood for some Cinema Verite kind of discussion. Anirban cut him short, 'Boss, can you help me with the tutorial on primitive societies? I have gone through the entire list of suggested readings. But I am getting nowhere,' he said.

Sharad put his thali on the table and eased himself into the chair. He then mixed the kadhi-chawal and planted the first spoonful in his mouth. 'This is great. You know, when you are hungry, even kadhi-chawal tastes like biryani. Missed the dinner last night due to the film show and overslept in the morning, so missed the breakfast too,' he digressed.

But only for a moment. 'No, I can't help you because I haven't read anything for that tutorial. Even if I had, I wouldn't have helped you. *Bhaiya, kisi bhale manas ne kaha tha, apna paikhana khud saaf karna padta hai.*' Which translated into the kindly advice that he should clean up his own shit.

Anirban wasn't prepared for this. 'Okay, thanks anyway,' he blurted out, hiding his disappointment.

As he turned to leave, Sharad asked him to sit down, 'Where are you going? Listen Anirban, you are looking for a crutch. Don't do that. Just work hard for six months. Put in more time than others in the library and everything will fall in place. There are no short cuts to anything.'

Anirban could see what Sharad meant. There was no other way out. This wasn't Ranchi University where one could cog from a friend's copy or get more marks simply by paying up the guys who mattered. He had to—what's the word?—improve himself.

'Just compare your problems with Sachin, your blind batchmate. Pay him a visit today and find out about his problems. Maybe then you will be able to see your own problems in a better perspective,' Sharad said.

Anirban had seen Sachin during the lectures. He was always ushered in by a helper of sorts. But he knew nothing about the guy. After the 3 p.m. lecture, he sought out Sachin.

'Hi Sachin, this is Anirban. Just wanted to come to your room after dinner and say hello.'

'Yaar, Monali is reading out to me till 9 p.m. Can you come after that?' he said.

'Sure.'

In Sachin's room, Anirban saw a pious-looking girl in a pink salwar-kurta read out from a sheaf of photostat copies. Anirban hadn't seen her before. But she seemed to be expecting him. 'Hi! I am Monali. Sachin told me that you would be coming around 9. Can I finish the last two pages before I go?'

'By all means,' Anirban replied. Monali continued reading out loud as Sachin kept listening intently. She was through in 10 minutes. 'I will be leaving now,' she said after the completing the chapter.

'Can you come around 7 in the evening tomorrow?' Sachin asked her.

'No. Tomorrow I am going to stay with my local

guardian. But I can come the day after for an hour. Would 8 p.m. be okay, Sachin?'

The blind boy nodded his head and smiled. 'Sure,' he said.

After Monali had left, Sachin said, 'Let us go and have some tea at the dhaba. We can chat there.'

Anirban wondered how a student who couldn't see would be able to write his term papers and take his examinations.

'Are the books you need available in Braille?' he asked Sachin.

'None. Not a single one,' he replied. 'Which is why I am dependent on friends like Monali. They read out the text to me. I make mental notes. Then I dictate the term paper.'

'But can Monali give so much of her time?'

'Of course not. Several students spare one or two hours every second day. That's how it is.'

'But I didn't see you taking down notes. How do you manage?'

'Well, when God takes away something from you, he also gives back something in return. I don't have my eyesight anymore. But my memory is good. If I concentrate hard enough, I remember,' he said.

Then he smiled and said, 'I have one major advantage. Being unable to see means there are no distractions. So I can focus on one thing at a time.'

'But how will you write the examinations?'

'The professors, even the administration, have been helpful so far. I will have a helper who will write down the answers I dictate. But tell me, why did you want to meet me?'

Anirban was speechless. He couldn't have possibly confessed that he had only come to find out if his own problems were worse than Sachin's.

'Where do you come from?' he asked Sachin, trying to change the subject.

'I come from a lower middle-class family in Barmer. Have you heard about it? It's a small town on the western edges of Rajasthan. I have some financial problems too. But the worse thing is the language barrier. You see, I went to Hindi-medium schools and colleges. Here every book is in English. So I have to first understand the language, then the jargon. I must remember everything, internalize it and then create a coherent argument which I again dictate in the form of a term paper.'

Anirban felt swamped by the sheer enormity of the obstacles before Sachin. There wasn't even a comparison between the two. He was amazed that Sachin didn't have an iota of self-pity. And even if he had, he was making a grand job of covering it to retain his dignity. He just seemed to have a genuine desire to learn, to get good grades and teach in a college. He wanted a better life for himself and was working towards it. Sachin wasn't letting hurdles hold him back; he was working around them to get ahead.

And here he, Anirban, was wallowing in self-pity.

'Why are you silent?' Sachin said, asking him a rather obvious question.

'Actually, I wanted to read out to you like the others.

I won't be able to give much time. But I can do one hour once a week,' Anirban said.

Sachin smiled. 'Pukka?' he asked.

'Pukka. I can come at 8 tomorrow,' Anirban replied.

'Great. I was wondering whom to approach for that evening slot,' he said.

8

Something to party

THE SENIORS IN CHS, as the history department was referred to, finally condescended to throw a fresher's welcome bash. It was two months too late. But nobody took such lapses seriously, especially a department that dealt with centuries and millenniums. As a return gift, the newcomers were asked to perform a variety show.

These revelries were as thrilling as watching Geoff Boycott bat. Even staring at sand falling in an hourglass was probably more rousing. Brawls were unheard of. Nobody made a pass. The only worthy memories of the old-timers were of drunken puking—sometimes in buckets that luckily happened to be around.

The variety show—'*Kuchh bhi kar dena yaar*, some jokes or something, *kucch bhi chalega*, does anybody play the guitar in your batch?'—was expected to bring some fun to an extremely avoidable tradition that deserved a quiet burial.

Unfortunately, nobody in Anirban's batch was remotely interested in that honourable objective. That was partly because seriousness was the most saleable and sought-after commodity in JNU. Everyone had come to believe that doing something as shallow and superficial as a skit or a music show could lead to the faculty perceiving you as a non-serious, lightweight student and consequently, your grades would be adversely affected. The facts of the case might have been different. But since when did facts come in the way of forming perceptions?

Anirban didn't care much about the faculty because he felt his plight couldn't get any worse. Some years back, he had been to the annual campus festival at IIT Kharagpur where he had seen some spoofs on popular ads. He thought they were rather good and could be replicated.

In one of them, a guy sitting on a commode makes a loud noise, then looks down. This is followed by the classic Jenson and Nicholson line: 'Whenever you see colour, think of us.' It wasn't exactly P.G. Wodehouse's idea of humour, but then JNU wasn't exactly uppity London either, right?

Another spoof was on the popular Surf ad with a fictional housewife named Lalitaji. In the actual campaign, Lalitaji compares two washing powders—obviously Surf turns out to be superior. *Bhala uski safedi meri safedi se behtar kaise* was the catch-line—triumphantly asserting the superior whiteness-endowing properties of Surf.

In the mimicked version, you saw two corpses wrapped in white sheets lying on the ground. One of them suddenly gets up and says, *Bhala uska kafan mere kafan se safed kaise*—an arguably hilarious scenario in which one corpse wonders why the other corpse's shroud is whiter than his.

Anirban wondered if he could rustle up a small group who could re-enact these spoofs. But the only batchmate who readily agreed to take part was Vandana, and for the strangest of reasons. 'I don't care what the faculty thinks of me. I am getting married next semester. And I might leave. What do you want me to do?' she asked. But gradually, he managed to cobble together a motley crew of willing performers.

Technically, the Open Air Theatre was located near the famous Parthasarthi plateau named after G. Parthasarthi, the first vice-chancellor of JNU. In reality, the OAT, as everyone called it, was in the middle of nowhere. A mythical Vishwamitra would have found this a suitable place to communicate with the gods or get seduced by a mythical Menaka.

One had to walk about 100 metres off the tar road and trudge through a territory overrun with hostile thorny bushes. Then you scrambled down a dirt trail for about 300 feet. It was obvious that the theatre was conceived by an anti-audience art designer determined to ensure that nobody ever watched a performance there. The plateau was also home to scorpions and snakes. But the truth is that it did not stop dozens of couples from making out in those challenging conditions every year. The moans made by lovers weren't always exultations of pleasure; sometimes they were just wails as pricks (the other kind) stung their backs.

Anirban's seniors had displayed a masochistic streak in hosting an event in this jungle of wild love. Nobody seemed to have offered much thought to the fact that most faculty members were on the wrong side of 50. Or, was this a sly revenge for all the B minuses and C pluses they lavished on students? Strangely, though, the entire faculty had taken up the challenge in good spirit. Almost everybody was present.

The show began after a brief welcome speech. Anirban couldn't believe his eyes when he saw most faculty members, some surprisingly overdressed in their Kanjeeravam silks, laugh with hysterical abandon.

After the show was over, Sharad was the first to walk up to Anirban and shake his hand. 'Bullseye,' he smiled. The show, it seemed, was a success for its sheer unacademicness. Everything in JNU was doused in politics and weighed down by political correctness. These skits were totally apolitical. That was reason enough to enjoy them. Perhaps its unapologetic levity reminded the faculty of a world they had long left behind.

Anirban had earned his 15 minutes of fame. It was like getting A+ in all term papers. He was pleasantly surprised to find two girls from the medieval India department walk up to congratulate him. For a moment, he thought they might even shake his hand. That they didn't disappointed him a little.

Anirban knew his world had changed when Niharika, the prima donna of the batch, walked up to him, fiddling with her yellow scarf, and said, rather haughtily, 'For some reason everybody seems to have liked your show. But I…'

She didn't get a chance to spew out the rest of her thoughts because the much venerated historian Ms Thapar interrupted her. 'Very imaginative, I must say. I really enjoyed it,' she winked at Anirban before walking away.

If nine words and a wink can change a young man's universe, this was it.

What Niharika was about to say became irrelevant because Ms Thapar had lavished her praise within earshot of other students. Niharika's minority report was meaningless now. Suddenly, she spotted an invisible hand beckoning her somewhere. 'Yeah…yeah…I am coming,' she said to no one in particular and moved to the other side of the OAT.

'Congratulations,' he heard a familiar voice soaked in sambhar say. It was Ms Kasturi, who else. 'Thanks,' he said, looking straight into her eyes for the first time since she had stepped into his room. Confidence born out of success, however trivial that success might be, had done that to Anirban.

'Excuse me…have you thought it over? I mean, have you decided about contesting?' It was Geetha Kasturi all right. She was looking right into his eyes. Eyes have a way of coming alive when something happy brews in the heart. Anirban wondered if he had seen that magical thing in Ms Kasturi's eyes or whether it was only his small-town imagination running away with him. *Maybe she is just an eager Commie*, he reasoned to himself.

There was no co-relation between Geetha's words and the way she looked. Her words were political and professional. But her body language—her upright posture, one hand on the hips and her breasts thrust forward almost in battleground position—seemed to tell a far more personal story.

Was she just talking or...*saying something*?

'Yes, I have. I am still undecided,' he said.

Geetha lurched closer. Anirban was sure if she moved even an inch forward, the buttons of his shirt would be saying hello to her nipples.

'Let us have dinner together,' she said.

Anirban could have been knocked down with a flying kiss.

'Where?' he fumbled like a kid promised an unexpected treat, and immediately regretted his shameful eagerness. Then, to parade his newfound confidence, he said, 'Hope the dinner conversation won't revolve around my potential candidature and the SFI's unending virtues.'

'Don't be so cocky,' she admonished him mildly, 'the SFI is going to win all the seats, with or without you.'

'Well, why are you investing time in me then?' he asked.

'I am not investing anything in you, not yet,' she smiled. 'Let us leave in 10 minutes.'

She had hardly finished her sentence when Robi walked up to Anirban and congratulated him. 'This was a masterstroke, man. Your winning chances just went up by 1000 per cent. Everybody in the history department knows you now. In JNU, everybody allegedly votes on ideology.

In the School of Social Sciences, people vote for the SFI by habit and tradition. It is almost like an injected drug in their brain. But you know, if they like you enough, they will make an exception. After all, you are not standing for the central panel but for a councillor's seat.'

My winning chances? Anirban asked himself. *When did I agree to contest?*

Deep in his heart, he knew that it wasn't right and rational on his part to fight the elections. Wasn't he in JNU to prepare for the civil services exams? He seemed to be falling into a trap that everybody had predicted he might.

But at the moment, politics was the last thing on his mind. Finishing his second glass of rum punch, Anirban sneaked away. He saw Ms Kasturi standing alone near a tamarind tree. Without exchanging words, they hurried out. It was dark. And Anirban was asking himself, *Should I make some kind of a move?* But, as usual, he didn't.

9

In the dark

'WHERE DO WE go?' asked Anirban.

'Let's go to Ganga dhaba,' she said.

Where else? Tea, coffee, nimboo-pani and bun-omelette—Ganga dhaba was the centre of JNU's culinary universe.

'I am no fan of its nimboo-pani,' Anirban complained. 'Have you seen the way they wash the glasses? And have you ever seen any Chhotu wash his hands? All of them are forever scratching themselves everywhere. And I am not sure of the quality of the ice either.'

'Gosh. Which country do you live in?' she was genuinely rebuking him.

'That's typically Leftist, right?' Anirban hit back. 'I talk hygiene and it becomes elitist.'

'Of course, it does,' Geetha wasn't backing off. 'If it is okay for most of JNU, it is good enough for you.'

'Of course, it is good enough for me. But that doesn't mean we cannot ask for better hygiene in the dhaba. Have you ever noticed the dogs licking the tea cups?'

'I have. And it doesn't bother me. They wash the cups, after all.'

'But have you seen how they wash them? They put all the cups in a bucket of water and take it out seconds later. No rinsing, no cleaning. And they use the same water the whole day.'

'God, you seem to be the sort who would ask his girlfriend to rinse her mouth before kissing.' Geetha was getting peevish.

'Not at all. I have never made such demands whichever part of the body I am kissing.' For once, Anirban was pretty ready for a scrap.

The bun-omelette arrived in a plate that looked like a relic from the Harappan Age. Geetha nearly winced before she realized that complaining would mean losing the argument. Anirban smiled. After the ideology-driven row, he felt a little more relaxed. Suddenly, he asked Geetha, 'Would you like to go and sit near the trees? It is so lit up here.'

Having said it, Anirban was surprised at his own audacity. He was even more surprised when Geetha loved the idea. 'Yeah, there is a small patch of grass that side,' she said, pointing towards a corner. 'I enjoy lying down there.'

Anirban was disappointed that she had already been there with someone else. But he made an Oscar-worthy job of concealing it.

On reaching the spot, Geetha fell to the ground, like a Hindi film heroine collapsing on a haystack, her arms and legs creating a T. When she turned around, she was smiling brightly at him, 'You are good at fighting with words,' she said. 'You will make a fine councillor candidate for the Free Thinkers.'

'But I am not a Free Thinkers' candidate,' he countered.

'No, you are not,' she replied cheerily. 'But you will soon be. Wanna bet on that?'

'I won't,' Anirban said. 'I don't bet.'

'See….and now that you have betrayed me,' she said with mock anguish, 'you must recite a poem to make me happy.'

'What kind of poem?'

'A poem that troubles you,' she said emphasizing the word *troubles*.

It doesn't take much for a small-town boy to lose his heart. And there, as he saw Geetha's face in the thin light of the dhaba bulb, he wondered if he was falling for her. The girls back home behaved like they were trophies to be won. But Geetha was different. She had individuality and a commitment to the cause she believed in. She was the first politically aware woman he had ever spoken to.

'I don't know if this poem will trouble you or not but it was the result of the poet's troubles,' he said. 'It is a love poem.'

'That's okay,' she said. 'Just don't recite the Neruda poem that ends with the line, "I want to do to you, what spring does to the cherry trees."'

'I wasn't going to recite that anyway. But why such an advance warning?'

'Well, I have heard it several times before. It is such a tender poem and the guys always make it sound like a pass.'

A ripple of jealousy surged through Anirban. He was troubled by her confessions. *Is she telling me that she is much sought after?* he asked himself. Thankfully, the darkness concealed his face, which had become a cardiograph of his heart.

'Well, you might consider this as a pass too. It is by a little known nineteenth-century English poet named Ernest Dowson. He fell in love with a waitress named Cynara. It went unrequited and his heart was shot to pieces. Dowson took to whoring and drinking. This poem is dedicated to Cynara, almost a sayonara in verse, pardon the pun. Here it goes:

> *Last night, ah, yesternight, betwixt her lips and mine*
> *There fell thy shadow, Cynara! Thy breath was shed*
> *Upon my soul between the kisses and the wine;*
> *And I was desolate and sick of an old passion,*
> *Yea, I was desolate and bowed my head:*
> *I have been faithful to thee, Cynara! In my fashion.*
> *I cried for madder music and for stronger wine,*
> *But when the feast is finished and the lamps expire,*
> *Then falls thy shadow, Cynara! The night is thine.*
> *And I am desolate and sick of an old passion,*
> *Yea, hungry for the lips of my desire:*
> *I have been faithful to thee, Cynara! In my fashion.*

'Very bourgeois but nice,' Geetha said, tucking a strand of hair that had strayed to her face, back to where it generally belonged.

'Very patronizing but thanks,' Anirban replied.

She laughed, almost admiringly, because Anirban had spotted the double-edged compliment. And then asked, 'Are you a romantic, Anirban?'

'I like to believe I am.'

'Well, I am quite the opposite of you then,' she said. 'I believe that romance is a bourgeois luxury. You cannot and should not love for love's sake.'

'So what does love mean to you?'

'I have never felt it deeply enough. I am being honest. I understand passion. But I really don't know what it is to be consumed by love.'

'What about the guys you have gone out with? Haven't you ever felt anything for anyone, something that makes you vertiginous, turns your universe upside down?'

Anirban had deliberately used the word 'vertiginous' having come across it in a *Time* magazine film review at the library. He was learning new words every day and had decided to try them out in conversations.

'For me, love isn't about finding someone attractive physically. I have never considered guys merely as workouts. You like a guy for what he is, what he stands for, the way he looks at society, interprets the world. I like people who are involved in changing things around them. It doesn't matter what or where. And it doesn't matter how much he succeeds. What matters is that he believes in something and that he tried. Once you start liking a guy like that, it doesn't matter how he looks. Frankly, it doesn't even matter whether he says I love you or takes you out for a romantic dinner. Such men make you feel alive. Which is why, though I would sympathize with a guy like your poet, I would find it hard to empathize with him. He is not, as one would say, my type.'

Anirban had long fantasized about having meaningful conversations with attractive women. Now, on an idle autumn night, he was finally having one.

'You seem to be confessing or suggesting that you don't believe in heart for heart's sake. You make love sound as though it is part of a larger mission. But love is not an appendage of ideology. When you think you love a certain kind of a guy for what he believes in, you actually don't love him but the idea he represents. You love him imagining him to be the man that you want him to be. That's not right because in your mind, you create a hero and a god. And when he falls short of your expectations, you feel let down. First you glorify him, then you crucify him.'

Geetha listened quietly without a word. Then, she gently took his hand into her own, and said, 'Let us say, Anirban, that our ideas on love are like parallel lines that don't meet. But I like your clarity.'

Anirban was touched, in more ways than one. 'Thanks for saying that. I like you too—for what you are, and wouldn't like to change any of that.'

They had finished dinner. Geetha wanted to leave. Anirban remembered he had to submit a term paper in Russian intellectual history. But he had a problem. The bulge in his pants was too pronounced. He had a tried and tested method of killing erections: Take a very deep breath and hold it for as long as you can. But how could he do that in front of Geetha? So he just sat down, pretending to tie his shoelaces. When he got up, the swelling had subsided but his walk was more erect than ever before.

10

Remembering Ma

THAT NIGHT WHEN he returned to his room, he saw a new message posted on the door of Room No. 22: *Marriage is like AIDS. Often you don't know you are carrying a fatal virus. Is this guy weird or married or both*? Anirban wondered.

On hitting the bed, Anirban suddenly remembered what his mother had told him outside the gate when he was leaving for Delhi. After he had touched her feet and was about to sit in the cycle rickshaw taking him to the railway station, she had said in that weak and meek voice, battered by decades of running a patriarchal household, 'Write letters regularly even if they are short. And please call once in a while.'

It had been days, indeed weeks since then, and he hadn't made that call. He had dropped a 15-paisa postcard in the rusty letter box near the bus stand the day he had arrived from Ranchi. 'Reached safely. Details in next letter', is all he wrote after that exhausting 32-hour journey on the Hatia–Amritsar Express. Most telegrams are longer.

Guilt, like anxiety, is a control freak. It takes hold of

everything you do. You want to flush it away from your body and mind. But it pulls you back, pins you down and ultimately drowns you.

That night a feeling of shame overwhelmed Anirban. He had not called home even once. The next feeling was of remorse. It made him miserable. He immediately rushed to the STD phone booth.

That the booth was open till 10.30 p.m. was being hailed as one of the great triumphs of the students' union. Everybody agreed that this was a technological revolution though most were unsure if it was a good thing or a bad thing for the campus.

JNU's basic instinct was anti-technology. The campus was subconsciously neo-Luddite in nature. Technology, best typified by computers, was deemed to be anti-poor and anti-people. They were tools of the rich and created to replace the workers, steal their jobs. That's what the Reds told you and what many had come to believe in.

Similarly, speaking to your parents or writing too frequently to them was a bourgeois hangover that needed to be minimized as much as possible.

For all the transformation, calling anybody back home was a major event which required careful planning. The stiff STD rates plunged to one-fourth after 9 p.m. This was the great discount zone when the vast majority of India got talking long distance if it had to. Consequently, the lines got jammed in no time. With only two STD booths open at night in the campus, there was always a long queue at the booths. Sometimes you had to wait for an hour and half.

Anirban wasn't the sentimental type but that day, for his mother's sake, he decided to stand in the queue as long as it took. The STD booth was located in an open area where a physically challenged woman sat behind a wooden table near the phone. To keep track and maintain order, she would hand out chits. Everyone waited patiently for his or her number. Nobody risked missing out on that joyful moment when his or her number was called out because it sent you back to the end of the queue.

Hearing your number being shouted out was sheer euphoria. Only a few things, like finding an hour of privacy with a willing girlfriend or discovering that the hostel loo was unoccupied during an urgent moment, could surpass that delight. Well, almost.

No conversations were private in the phone booth. Words of anguish, terms of endearment and declarations of love—all were made within the earshot of a dozen or more fellow students. The phone booth was certainly no place for the inhibited.

As he inched ahead in the queue, reading the rough draft of a tutorial on Gandhi's methods of mobilization he had written in the afternoon, Anirban could overhear a girl from Orissa, judging by her accent, tell her mother that she was missing home-cooked food and her pet dog, Toffee. But he couldn't understand a word of what the next guy said. Was he from Kerala or Andhra Pradesh? For a moment, he marvelled at India's diversity.

Then he heard the guy mention 'Marilyn Monroe' a couple of times. *Who's he talking to? What kind of a guy discusses Ms Monroe in a STD booth where people are waiting to find out about their ailing parents or dying cats or whatever?* For a moment, he felt like gunning down the bastard.

There was no telephone at Anirban's home. To talk to his parents, he had to call Khan Uncle who lived in the neighbourhood. They would send someone to his parents with the message. The phone would be on hold for at least five minutes before he could resume the call. Anirban usually had two options—make a second call, which meant going back in the queue and waiting for another hour; or, just hold on and burn money. But that night, all he heard on the phone was a persistent message: *All lines in this route are busy.*

He returned to the hostel guilt-free. At least he had tried. Anirban knew his parents loved him more than he deserved. He respected his father for the man he was: an honest police officer who was forced to scrounge for work in insurance companies after retirement.

His childhood lacked the kind of drama that would fire up a screenplay writer of melodrama. An unhappy day meant being refused money to watch the latest Rajesh Khanna movie. A happy occasion meant going to Hong Kong, the Chinese restaurant, with his parents where the order never changed: two by three chicken sweetcorn soup, two chicken chowmein and one chilli chicken.

But after his father's retirement five years back, everything changed. His parents never discussed this but he knew that every month ended in a painful struggle between needs and desires. They were always short of cash in the last week of the month, which always ended with variations of potatoes and spinach in every meal. Those seven days or so passed by in super slow motion. Anirban could almost watch every hour crawl past them as if they were mocking his fate. There is no bigger deprivation than suddenly being pushed down the social ladder.

Occasionally, he would notice his father switch off the lights almost mechanically and haggle with vendors over the price of vegetables. He had never done these things before. And he didn't know how to do it.

In Anirban's eyes, his father was always the big guy; the man who barked orders at sub-inspectors and orderlies. He always looked like a guy in control of his life, his surroundings. To watch him fight petty battles, and sometimes even lose them, was painful. He couldn't bear to see it.

He knew he had hardly been a model son. Far from it, he had been unreasonable. His father's retirement required a change in the family's lifestyle, a lowering of expectations of what could be provided and what had to be avoided. Anirban understood that. But understanding is one thing. Behaving accordingly is an entirely different matter.

In his college days, Anirban would shout at his mother for the most trivial of reasons. Once, after a bitter fight with his father over pocket money, he had left home and stayed at a friend's for a few days. He returned when his father came to fetch him after finding out where he was. He had savoured the moment as one of personal triumph. Now he knew it was immature of him to have done that.

He regretted leaving his home that day, though he could never get himself to admit it to his parents.

I am past that reckless, unreasonable phase, Anirban thought as he lay down on his bed. But he still wasn't at all sure if he was on the same page with his parents.

All his life as a police officer, his father had watched district collectors at close quarters. Like many fathers, he wanted his son to achieve what he hadn't. Like most middle-class parents in Bihar, he too, firmly believed that *Upar Bhagwan hai aur neeche IAS hai*—God rules above and IAS below.

His parents had never spelt out upfront what they wanted from him but Anirban was aware of their unsaid wish. The random conversations he had with his friends and seniors were coming back to haunt him. He had been dismissive of them then. Now he realized he was just being cocky.

It was way past midnight when Anirban heard a knock on the door. He had a good mind to tell whoever it was to buzz off.

It was Robi. 'Come to the basketball court tomorrow at 10 p.m. We will announce the name of the FT candidates. You are one of them, right?'

'No!' Anirban wanted to scream. 'Yeah. Okay,' he mumbled resignedly.

11

The election

MOST COLLEGES, UNIVERSITIES and other institutes have cultural festivals every year. JNU had a rousing campus carnival for the politically inclined: the student's union elections. The annual students' union poll was a wonder of electoral democracy that defined the university's distinct personality.

Everything about the election was incredibly civilized. No involvement of the university administration. No cops. No use of money or muscle. The Election Commissioner was a senior student; someone regarded as neutral and honourable by all parties. Open spaces in the campus were marked out for posters and distributed equally among the parties.

For those like Anirban who had come from Bihar, any election involving students was unthinkable without a few incidents of stabbing or someone getting his bones rearranged. *These elections must be totally bland*, he told himself.

Anirban turned up at the basketball court rather late.

But nobody seemed to notice or care. The mood was more party than political. In one corner, a small group of older students was inhaling something regarded as mandatory on such joyous occasions—you could tell by the shape of the cigarette, the smell in the air and the relaxed calm in their voices. Elsewhere, a senior was cracking extremely sad jokes with a group of freshers. They were laughing: it wasn't clear whether at the jokes or at him.

'The great news is that the Free Thinkers will be contesting allllll seatssss,'—this was Robi, sloshed and slurring.

The news was hailed as some kind of Old Testament miracle since it hadn't happened for some years. Two seniors, Mastana Singh and Robi, were singled out for praise for working selflessly and tirelessly. In simpler terms, for their ability to attract fresh fish.

Yogendra Kishore for president and Manoj Mahapatra for general secretary—that was the choice and everybody seemed to approve it. It was not clear who had selected them in the first place. The selection process seemed a little opaque to Anirban. But the names of all candidates for the central panel as well as the councillor candidates were met with loud drunken cheers.

The general view was that the party had found the right balance of gender and geography for most panels, except in the School of Social Sciences where the list was all male: two tall Biharis, one short Oriya, one balding bloke from AP and, rather oddly, a frail Bengali from Bihar, who was Anirban.

When his name was announced, everyone lined up to congratulate him. 'If you play your cards right, both Biharis and Bengalis will vote for you. I guarantee that,' one of the party's ideologues declared. He was so emphatic that Anirban felt obligated to win the election only to prove him right.

'How do regional considerations matter? I thought only ideology mattered in JNU.' Anirban told Jack later.

'Don't be naïve,' Jack snubbed him. 'Ideology matters at one level. But when you are contesting an election, you cannot ignore other social realities. We don't have the caste factor here. And as long as the ABVP or the Jamaat don't find a foothold, religion will not be a factor either. In fact, the Muslims generally vote en bloc for the SFI because they are constantly told by the SFI that we are keeping the ABVP away from the campus.

'But regional bias is an important factor in a national university. And with so many girl students, you must have proper representation of women to be gender-friendly. You have to be a good speaker too. The JNU is a Red bastion. Like blind mice, most cadres will queue up before the booth on polling day. But many are also anti-SFI in the campus. Some are pathologically averse to the Left. Those guys will vote for us because we are the number one opposition party. But our job is also to catch the floating votes, of the neutral and the apolitical. If we manage to catch a majority of the floating votes and the anti-SFI vote, we win.'

'If you are talking about good speakers, how come Manoj Mahapatra is on the central panel?' Anirban said.

'I know he has a pipsqueak voice. But the Oriyas are the single largest community in JNU. There are about 450 Oriya votes. You would need about 800 votes to win a seat in the central panel. Manoj is very well networked among Oriyas. Let us see if the SFI has an Oriya candidate in its central panel. If they don't have one, he will not only sail through but will also pull in the Oriya votes for Yogendra.'

'What calculations!' Anirban couldn't help exclaiming.

'Yes. That's elections, at whatever level. And there's nothing you can do about it. See, the SFI will also try to distribute their candidates to suit their primary voters. You will see they will have at least two Muslims in their School of Languages' councillor panel. That's because they are aiming at the votes of the Muslim students from Arabic Studies.'

After the announcements, Jack gave a brief motivational speech. 'We don't owe our allegiance to any political party outside. We don't believe that all problems of the world can be solved on the basis of a book written in the nineteenth century.'

'What book is he talking about?' a newcomer asked Robi.

'*Das Kapital*, genius,' he glowered.

Jack continued, 'We have gathered here to discuss the students' union election which takes place exactly 21 days from now. The SFI has been winning for the past two years and has done nothing. There is a huge anti-SFI and anti-incumbency mood and we must exploit it as much as we can.

'We have already formed all the committees for the election. There is a poster committee, a pamphlet committee, a meeting committee. From now onwards, we will organize meetings in different hostels every night. Each of you should not only be present in these meetings but also get as many of your friends to attend them. The councillor candidates in every school will be guided by a campaign co-ordinator. He will plan and organize your schedule.

'As Free Thinkers, for the next 21 days, you are all going to eat, drink and sleep elections. We can do it this time. We can. And we will.'

As he finished, two slogans boomed in the air, 'Free Thinkers march on!' and 'Ho Ho, Ho Chi Minh, they shall fight, we shall win!' The second one was with tongue firmly in cheek.

The names of the campaign co-ordinators were announced by Robi. Each co-ordinator was to be assisted by two girl students whose main job was to introduce the candidates to female hostellers. Barring hostel nights, guys weren't allowed inside girls' hostels.

Anirban and the four other FT councillor candidates from the School of Social Sciences—Rajesh Dubey, Aviral Patnaik, Nandu Sinha and Venugopal Rao—were introduced to Amarnath Biswal, the co-ordinator of their campaign.

Biswal had spent five years studying Durkheim and his theory of suicide. 'Contesting on a FT ticket in the School of Social Sciences is as good as political suicide,' he joked, unable to move away from his PhD topic.

Then he quickly switched channels, 'I really believe we can make a breakthrough this time. But for that we must be prepared to work real hard. My job is to prepare you for the campaign. I have to motivate you, keep your chin up when the chips are down. For starters, let's meet exactly at 8 a.m. tomorrow and catch the students on the ground floor of the SSS building before they enter their classrooms for the morning lecture,' he said.

The enormity of the situation now dawned on Anirban. It was obvious that he had to either bid lectures goodbye for the next three weeks, or, make a mockery of himself as a candidate. He realized he was doing everything that he swore never to fall for. He felt weightless and rootless; someone without any sense of his own ground.

Next morning at breakfast he met Sharad. 'So you got bullied into contesting the election?' he said.

'You are bang on target,' Anirban admitted admiringly.

'People who do not know who they are and what they want out of life are generally taken advantage of. You are not a political guy so why are you jumping into politics?' Sharad was direct, maybe even a little savage.

Then he eased up, 'I don't think there's any major harm in contesting the elections. Look at the worst-case scenario. You will lose and get C in a couple of term papers. But it will be great exposure for you. You will understand a few things about politics and a few things about people. I suggest, forget term papers and certainly don't think about the civil services in the next few weeks. Just focus on the elections. But say goodbye to politics after the polls, especially if you think you are not cut out for it.'

As the two stepped out of the mess room, Anirban was intercepted by a tall student who was always covered up in a hoodie.

'Great, boss. I heard you are contesting elections,' he started off. 'See, canvassing during elections gives you the legitimate right to chat up any girl, shake her hand. Overall, if you say hello to 500 girls during the campaign, and even five are impressed, your target is achieved.' He backslapped Anirban before walking away.

Aside from thanking him, Anirban wanted to see his face but couldn't.

When Anirban reached the SSS building, he only had Nandu for company. By a coincidence, the SFI panel was also campaigning there. Anirban looked for Geetha but she wasn't around. 'Where are the others?' Biswal asked.

'I don't know,' he shrugged.

By the time, the full panel had arrived, it was almost 8.30. A majority of students had already entered the classrooms. The others were hurrying in.

'We are late. No need to waste time here. Let us go to the library gate and campaign there,' Biswal said.

The students who were arriving early appeared to be the super serious types. They were either indifferent, or hostile to the campaigners. Some muttered a feeble hello, eager to get over the conversation as quickly as a rectal examination.

Others would brush past them, 'Yaar, I have a term

paper and running late.' A few would say, 'Okay. I vote for the Free Thinkers anyway.' But a few would be brusque and contemptuous, 'Free Thinkers? Never. Free from thinking, that's what you guys are.'

Biswal would be equally contemptuous of this lot. 'Arrey, these are SFI *paltus*, pets, you know. They are the ones who have mortgaged their minds to Marx. They will never vote for you, even if you know them personally. So fuck these guys. Why waste your time? Remember, we are looking for the floating votes, the freshers who have not been brainwashed by the SFI cadres. Even when you are eating breakfast, lunch or dinner, feel free to chat up people. In the end, not everybody votes for ideology. You can always squeeze out a personal vote, if not for the entire panel, if you know a guy well enough.'

Anirban and others nodded mournfully. The morning hadn't gone according to plan and the spirit was generally low. But Biswal had perked up everybody by say, 20 per cent. Under the circumstances, that was an awful lot.

At lunch, they visited the Kaveri Mess, a bit of a Free Thinkers' den. The response was positive. Jack, the king of free gyan, was there. 'Don't waste time on us. We are all there for you. Just try to ensure that everybody's personal vote becomes a panel vote. Every friend of Anirban should not only vote for him but for the entire panel. Nandu should ensure that all his friends vote for the entire panel. If you can translate every friend's vote into a panel vote, then you guys have a decent chance. Remember, SFI voters are panel voters because they vote on the basis of ideology, not for the candidate. Even if they have a duffer as a candidate, which they always have in plenty, they will vote for him. Our case is different. We don't have too many panel voters. Our campaigning is basically about creating panel voters,' he said.

As they were about to leave, Jack stopped them, 'One more thing. I know there is no girl in your panel. That's a major weakness. Because a girl can approach other girls easily. She can also campaign in the girls' hostels. But stay confident. Canvassing is a game of confidence. Even if a girl ignores you or behaves rudely, don't take it personally. It is part of the game. Remember, persistence pays. Even if you have spoken to someone once, don't hesitate to do it again. And don't forget, for everybody the sweetest sound in the world is someone calling out his or her name. Try to remember as many names as possible. It works wonders because it boosts your ego to be recognized and be sought out by others.'

Anirban made a mental bookmark of that last line. In the afternoon, as they stood outside the Godavari girls' hostel, he was brave enough to stop a few students and ask for a minute of their time. Some said, 'I am sorry, not interested.' But a few listened to them, perhaps out of politeness, as they asked for their 'vote and support'.

Initially, he felt bad when a girl responded brusquely. But after a few times, he started enjoying the game. He realized that canvassing was all about maintaining poise and cool, no matter how much one was provoked. The refusals didn't matter as long as he was able to balance them with some positive responses too.

Anirban managed to make an impression on Pushpa Kerketta. A PhD student in the School of Life Sciences, she was from Bokaro, the steel town about 150 kilometres from Ranchi. So there was a connection of sorts. She smiled good-naturedly as Anirban conversed with her. After she had left, Anirban announced, '*Iska to vote pucca.*'

Biswal wasn't satisfied, '*Tera vote pucca hoga, par poora panel ka vote pucca chahiye*, including the central panel. Invite her for the Free Thinkers' meeting tonight. Make her feel like a special invitee. That's how you get votes.'

Anirban shouted out to her. She stopped and looked back, puzzled. When he invited her to the meeting, she seemed reluctant. 'I work in the lab, yaar. I don't understand politics at all.' Anirban was cool. 'I am not asking you to waste time over politics. I just wanted you to meet our presidential candidate. If you want to leave immediately after that, it is up to you,' he smiled. It was not exactly a plea, more an invitation.

'What time?' she asked.

'9.30 p.m.'

'Okay. I will see.'

By 3 p.m., Anirban felt he had walked a 100 kilometres and spoken to about a million students. In reality, he might have walked five and spoken to 50. He felt drained. He came to realize that political campaigning is a great deal of physical work and, for a moment, marvelled at the energy of the politicians who campaigned 18 hours a day, sometimes delivering six speeches in three different towns over 24 hours.

He also realized pretty early that two candidates in their panel, Rajesh and Aviral, did not have their hearts in the campaign. They neither had the inclination nor the desire to win. They behaved as if they had done the party a favour by offering to become candidates. Nandu, on the other hand, was committed, but only to his own cause. He behaved as if he had been chained to a group that was holding him back and pulling him down. Nandu looked eager to, as they say, plough the lone furrow.

But Anirban had taken his unofficial mentor Sharad's words to heart: Give it a good shot. And then forget all about it. At night, he introduced Pushpa to FT's presidential candidate Yogendra Kishore and the rest of the central panel. She seemed wide-eyed about the whole thing. After a while, she excused herself, saying she had to go to the lab.

But Jack looked impressed by Anirban's efforts. 'Did you know her from back home?'

'No,' he replied.

'Then you have understood rather quickly what canvassing is all about. This girl is going to vote for us. You know why? Because you have valued her. And she will return the favour with her vote. That's how you do it. Make friends. Don't look at prospective voters as *bakras*. Be sincere. It matters,' Jack said even as he moved towards a gang of hesitant first-year girls who appeared to have just strayed in out of curiosity.

The meeting was over by 11 p.m. Anirban was so tired, he could have crashed on the floor. But something kept nagging him through the day, even while he was shaking hands with unknown students outside the classrooms and inside the canteens.

Ms Kasturi was a persistent presence in his thoughts. At times, he would look around hoping to find her among one of the girls walking by. Anirban realized he was thinking about her more than he wanted to.

And he found himself walking towards the Sutlej hostel, hoping to find Geetha there. He had heard the SFI was hosting their evening meeting there. The Sutlej mess room was packed like a cricket stadium where some bearded Commie was breathing fire like a dragon on heat. The hall was also filled with smoke because like everyone else on the stage, he was also puffing at his Charms cigarette.

'Our struggle is the struggle of the working class across the globe. We are fighting for the farmers in the fields, for the workers in the factories, for the unemployed millions in the streets. The day is not far off, when this rotten system will come crashing down.' Thunderous cheers were followed by the slogan—SFI, March On!—and the echo of the cadres, *March on, March on.*

Revolution, it seemed, was knocking on the doors of India and most likely was going to happen by the weekend.

Anirban spotted Geetha and he thought their eyes met. But she did not make any effort to move towards him. He left, a trifle downcast and dejected. The heart is an unreasonable creature—and it was misbehaving with him at the moment.

When he reached the hostel room, the light was

switched off and the door was locked from inside. He could hear the hurried rustle of clothes and the back door open and shut in quick succession. Then Bhatia opened the front door. '*Yaar, meri Roosi gudiya ko padha raha tha*, I was really busy teaching my Russian doll,' he explained, rather unnecessarily.

'With the light off? ' Anirban said, trying to keep sarcasm out of his voice.

'We fell asleep while studying,' Bhatia said, without batting an eyelid.

Half-dead, Anirban was in no position to interrogate him further. He hit the bed without taking off his shoes. And was gone in 60 seconds.

12

The sanctuary

ON THE THIRD day of the campaign, Anirban discovered the real JNU elections. In the afternoon, they were campaigning door-to-door, literally in this case, in Poorvanchal, a hostel so removed from the rest of the campus, you felt it was like a retreat.

Poorvanchal was the lair of the veterans. Some of them had dawdled on their PhDs for nearly a decade and had turned themselves into campus fossils. Their stories always began with the line, 'In our days…' They were the badshahs of late-night debates that continued till the rum and cigarettes were finished. They were legends in their own mind. You could say they had been institutionalized.

Biswal, Anirban's campaign co-ordinator, had filled them in on Poorvanchal, how and why the hostel needed a different style of campaigning.

'Many of these students should have completed their PhD years ago and left. But for one reason or other, they either didn't or couldn't. Many of them neither have the willpower nor the ability to face the world. Which is why you have got to be extra careful. You have to boost their egos. Meet everyone with extra humility as if you are meeting Mahatma Marx in person. Treat each of them like God's gift to the world of intellect and you will be fine.'

Poorvanchal was easily the toughest hostel to negotiate, Anirban soon realized. Some rooms had curt yellow notes posted outside the door: Vote Seekers Stay Away. A few of them appeared to have been locked for months. A couple of those who condescended to open the room, said rather pompously, 'This is no time to disturb senior scholars. Don't you know I sleep in the afternoon?'

However, the occupant of Room No. 208 welcomed them in. Moments after sitting on his bed, they realized he was sloshed. 'I tell you guys, JNU died in the summer of 1983. There's nothing left here. What goes on in the name of students' election is a sham. Can anyone debate like Jairus Banaji and D.P. Tripathi today?' he asked nobody in particular.

Anirban and everyone else were expecting a long speech from him. But suddenly the gentleman fell silent and started gazing at the ceiling. They all trooped out.

Another hosteller was equally eccentric. 'Okay. I will vote for you guys if you answer my question in the next 30 seconds. Can you name two books written by Herbert Marcuse?'

Nandu was quick to pounce on that. '*One-Dimensional Man* and *Escape from Freedom*,' he said.

'Good. Now can you say something about his work?' He wasn't the easy-to-please type.

Venugopal responded with exaggerated deference. 'Sir, let me try. In *One-Dimensional Man*, Marcuse tells us how people begin to identify themselves with the commodities they buy. They begin to look for their souls in their cars and music systems. He is suggesting that under capitalism, humans become extensions of the material goods they purchase.'

'Good,' replied the rather middle-aged student, puffing intermittently at an unlit beedi while holding a lungi hitched up to the knees with his other hand. 'That means the new lot of students isn't as bad as they have been telling us. Give us your names. I will vote for you guys. The SFI guys had come here yesterday and they were able to give just one name. That's why I am losing faith in the Communists.'

They left, pleased. 'Will he vote for us?' Anirban asked Amarnath.

'You bet, he will.'

But there is something to worry about,' Anirban said. There was a furrow of anxiety in his voice.

'What?' Nandu asked.

'That the SFI has been here before us. You know, it is a bit like getting the attention of a girl. It is generally first come, first selected. The best candidates often lose out because they wait too long thinking about the outcome. It is the same with elections, too.'

By evening, Anirban felt like a dog that had been beaten beyond endurance. He had been asked to assemble in the election control room where senior FTs allegedly worked on strategies, if there was such a thing. Far from it, the room was full of young students like him though they gave the impression of being much happier with their lives than he was.

The control room had been borrowed from a FT sympathizer, a senior student in sociology out on a field trip to Cuddalore in Tamil Nadu. The room was well-maintained except for the fact that the man, for some strange reason, seemed to have a fetish for dinosaurs. The wall was pasted with their posters.

Petulant slogans were being put to paint on chart paper. This was instant political art. Three girls and a nerdy boy were working on the posters. In the balcony, someone was writing the next day's pamphlet, while his girlfriend, or so it seemed, was playing an imaginary sitar on his thighs. Someone was making tea. Mastana, feted as FT's top organizer and recruiter the other night, looked to be their mentor, having drawn these first-year students to the party's fold.

One girl dressed in a careless, casual yellow top and light blue jeans, Anirban noticed, looked like a hotline to heaven.

Mastana introduced him to her. She was Nivedita Jha, a second-year student of Spanish. Anirban immediately regretted not having read anything on Lorca, the poet of love and despair killed in the Spanish civil war. And he almost slapped himself for refusing a book of his translated poems from a friend back in Ranchi.

But as the night wore on, he found himself getting

increasingly drawn towards a quiet dusky girl in the far corner of the room. Anirban found her totally immersed in her work, hardly saying a word to anybody else in the room. She seemed untouched by the surroundings as if mentally she was some place else. Somehow, she didn't fit in with the rest of the crowd.

'Who is that in the corner?' Anirban asked Mastana as they stepped out for a smoke.

'That's Purnima Kumari from Arrah. Our best artist. Her life has been pretty tragic, you know. From what I have heard, she was married off at a young age but her husband died of TB. Her in-laws wanted her to get married to his younger brother. When she refused, they imprisoned her in a room. But she managed to run away. She hid herself in the railway station before taking a midnight train to her home 200 kilometres away.'

'It was all very filmi, I am told. Apparently, she had no money and locked herself in a toilet during the journey. But she was determined to start a new life. I don't know how she got to know about JNU, but she came prepared for the long haul. She spent six months as an illegal guest with a friend in Godavari and somehow got through the entrance test. In fact, she is one batch senior to you. The professors like her because she has shown spunk in real life and beaten the odds. She is also amazingly talented. Her charcoal drawings are top-class, very original. You will see she is one of the finest poster artists in the campus.'

Anirban wondered why he hadn't noticed Purnima before. Was she present at the freshers' party? Had she seen his infantile skit?

Some posters were ready by the time they had finished their tea. Indeed, they were top-drawer. Clean, confident lines drawn with flourish and feel. Mastana asked a couple of girls to accompany him. 'Why don't you too come along?' he asked. Anirban was tired but the girls were attractive, or so he thought, though Nivedita and Purnima weren't among them. He agreed, taking care not to show extra enthusiasm.

Just as they were stepping out, another girl entered the room. She was wearing a black T-shirt and a floral skirt that failed to camouflage her burgeoning hips. Mastana immediately lit up like a Christmas tree. 'Hello Usha, we were all waiting for you,' he lied.

Putting up posters was nothing less than an erotic adventure, Anirban realized. For Usha and Mastana, it certainly was. Posters brushed with glue by Anirban were gently handed over to Usha. She would then hold them in her hands and sit on Mastana's substantial shoulders, putting her legs on either side of his head. The latter would then slowly stand up on wobbling legs, much like a weightlifter trying to lift kilos beyond his strength. Usha would then stick the posters high on the wall.

The reason for doing this, Mastana explained, was that the posters must be out of reach of anybody interested in tearing them off. And, it appeared, there were many. 'But why don't we find a ladder to do this?' one of the girls asked. Mastana mumbled something about shortage of funds and the fact that a ladder would be of no use after a fortnight.

'I don't mind at all. Glad to help the party in whatever way possible,' said Usha cheerfully.

As they slapped dozens of posters in different areas of the campus, Anirban imagined swapping positions with Mastana though he wasn't physically up to the task. *Elections can be real fun, if you are involved in doing the right things*, he thought.

After finishing with the posters, they sat down for another round of tea at Ganga dhaba. Anirban was surprised when he saw Geetha walk up to him. 'Hi! How's the campaign coming along?'

'So far, so good,' he replied. 'Have you met my friends? This is Usha and that's…'

'I know Mastana. Everybody in the campus knows Mastana Singh,' she replied, smiling rather mysteriously. She wasn't exactly complimenting him.

And then he remembered that he was meeting Geetha for the first time since his name had been announced as a Free Thinker candidate. He was surprised she didn't say anything about that; after all, she had been trying hard to make him join the SFI. And she had predicted he would be contesting the elections even when he himself was not so sure.

'Let us meet tomorrow at 7 p.m. outside Kaveri hostel,' she said, out of the blue.

'I will try,' Anirban replied meekly.

'You must be busy. But I will wait for you,' she said, and left abruptly.

'Why does she want to meet you at 7 p.m. tomorrow?

Doesn't she know that you are in the middle of a campaign? I think she is just trying to divert your attention. Because they know that you are a strong candidate,' Mastana said.

'You are imagining things. She was just being friendly. The SFI doesn't need a Mata Hari to defeat me,' Anirban replied tersely.

'She is a smart girl and very dedicated to the SFI. Just remember one thing: comrades fall in love with comrades. And comrades marry comrades. That is the way it is. That is the only way they find happiness. Whenever they marry anyone outside the caste of communism, it becomes a half-baked relationship. If you are interested in her, just watch out.'

Anirban felt that Mastana was being paranoid. But he also knew that there was an iota of truth in his last words,

13

The debate

As THE V-DAY came closer, the pamphlets got more pompous, the slogans bolder and the campaigning frenetic.

Old timers said the campaigns in the 1970s and early 1980s focused more on international than national or local issues. Speeches were delivered on securing justice for Palestine, expressing solidarity with Nelson Mandela and highlighting evil America's excesses. It was certainly easier to debate on Mogadishu's malnutrition than promise an extra hour of water for the hostels and being held accountable for that unfulfilled promise a year later.

Now it was more national. Only the NSUI focused on campus problems and was summarily dismissed as a party with a municipal vision of the world. On this, there was near-unanimity among the Lefties of different hues.

This was also the time when every party brought out a manifesto. Nobody knew how many students read them. But the manifestos were solemn, self-important works. In four small pages, they fleshed out every party's political stand on national and international issues of consequence.

Every manifesto was a tirade against the university authorities. For every party, the JNU administration was the immediate class enemy. This is what every student was brainwashed into believing as soon as he or she stepped into the campus. In the unionist narrative, the authorities were always trying to encroach upon student's rights. Every move made by them was an intrigue against students.

The manifesto mattered. You had to defend your stated position and withstand intense interrogation in the public meetings. The Free Thinkers' manifesto, written by Jack, was a rehash of what had been written the year before. And the year before. But it was okay: they, too, were written by Jack.

If an election was JNU's grand social event, the presidential debate was its showstopper, the prom night of the campus. Even the old fogies from Poorvanchal who hadn't stepped out of their hostels for months, the library-addicts and the civil services types who had mastered the art of taking a bathroom leak in 15 seconds to save time, would emerge from the woodwork to spend a late night at the Jhelum lawns.

For many, the night of the presidential debate announced the arrival of winter. It was the night when everyone pulled out their coats, woollen jackets, pullovers and shawls from the embarrassingly plebeian aluminium trunks.

The FT's presidential candidate could pip the SFI to the post. That was the buzz in the campus. Even Sharad, a radical Left sympathizer, admitted to Anirban that

Yogendra could come out tops because there was anger against the 'sarkari' Left regime and an acute sense of disappointment over the SFI's performance in the union. 'Maybe because they have won for the past two years and the students want a change,' he said.

As a speaker, Yogendra was no Mario Cuomo, that silver-tongued orator of the US Democrats, but he packed too many punches for SFI man Buddhadeb Basu. Buddhadeb was a Marlboro Marxist of the finest variety but lacked the earthy appeal of Yogendra. The rumour was that he had been preferred over a far more deserving and hard-working candidate because his father was a close friend of a CPM politburo member. In other words, he was part of the Commie aristocracy. But even the SFI's star campaigners such as the suave and sharp-witted former JNUSU president Sitaram Yechuri could do little to improve his chances.

FT's general secretary candidate, Manoj Mahapatra, was also in the running but he was up against a talented student of economics, Nidhi Khullar, who incidentally had an Oriya boyfriend. Manoj's chances, campus psephologists insisted, had suffered because a significant number of Oriya votes were likely to be divided between the two. She was not only expected to get the combined votes of the SFI–AISF cadres but also of the frusto crowd—short form for the sexually frustrated.

'She shook my hand. I will vote for her all my life,' a Sutlej hostel old-timer told Manoj. He laughed uproariously when Manoj offered to do the same.

Those who made up their mind at the last moment, voted on the basis of a candidate's performance during the late night, open air show. The candidates were given about 15 minutes to make their speech and had to respond to questions from the audience later.

The SFI–AISF supporters were made to sit strategically among the rest of the audience. Like unpaid claques, they cheered or hooted, depending on who was speaking. The other part of their job was to fling awkward bouncers to the rivals and gentle full-tosses to their own. Barring newcomers, nobody got taken in by the antics.

This was the Ganga dhaba's biggest night too. The dhaba stayed open till the debate ended, which often stretched past 2 a.m. The tea and the coffee would get more and more watery with every passing hour. Everybody noticed that but nobody cared. Students would queue up for the insipid chai through the night.

Discussions primarily, and understandably, would centre on the quality of the ongoing debate. Old-timers would invariably lament its falling standards. Anecdotes from the great debates of the past were recounted with great relish. How a FT candidate spent two minutes discussing the quality of potatoes in the mess when the opposition was talking about Cuba and how he set a record for the lowest number of votes for a Free Thinker.

Many students genuinely believed that the JNUSU debate had more quality and passion than the US presidential debates. It's another matter that none of them had either seen or heard the US debates. It was part faith, part pride, part prejudice. Not all of them were Reds who held that view. Right or wrong, this was the self-perception of the campus.

This was also the night of the great rendezvous. Hostels would empty out during the debate and the security would be relatively lax. Lovers would grab the opportunity, literally and figuratively, with both hands to slip into the rooms. For once, you could make a front-door entry.

On the stage that night, Yogendra outsmarted his rival Buddhadeb. He blamed the SFI for everything under the sun—the years of misrule in West Bengal, the state government's mishandling of the Gorkhaland agitation, the flaws of Communist USSR, the poor state of the DTC bus service. Probably, even the failure of the monsoon. But he spoke with a sense of authority.

'You know the SFI will tell you that politics is an agency for something bigger than all of us. They want to change the world. I say, of course. I understand the importance of taking a stand on every political issue that confronts us. But I also say: don't forget the backyard. Listening to them, one feels it is easier to change the world than the campus. I want to know why issues such as increasing the frequency of buses, more merit-cum-means scholarship for more students and more hours of water in hostels figure so low in their list of priorities. If they can't improve our lives in the campus, how can they speak of making the world a better place?' Yogendra spoke to applause.

It looked as if he had swayed the neutral ones to his side. And even the practised jeers of the cadres could not alter that.

But the night saw the rise of an unlikely challenger: the NSUI's Mohit Shivalkar. In JNU, NSUI candidates were generally as important as fast bowlers in the Indian cricket team of the early 1970s.

But Shivalkar had some game-changing features on his résumé. He had acted in a DD serial and sincerely believed that only two persons could outdo him in the looks department: Shashi Kapoor and Robert Redford. It helped that neither of them was a student in the campus.

He also had a gravelly voice and a gift for rapid repartee. When asked about the role of the Congress in initially propping up the Khalistan movement, he posed a counter-question: 'Tell me which party has sacrificed its top leader fighting communalism?'

He continued, 'When Mrs Gandhi asked the army to go inside the Golden Temple, she knew she was taking a potentially life-threatening decision; but she did it for the sake of the country.' The answer obfuscated the complexity of the separatist problem in Punjab. But that night, it was a great answer to a tricky question. Shivalkar got a busload of cheers; and not all of them were from the NSUI supporters b(r)ought from Delhi University.

During the hectic campaign, Anirban had come across Geetha a couple of times but both were too pre-occupied with their separate lives to talk at leisure. During the debate too, he kept looking for Geetha in the crowd but wasn't able to spot her. *Where is she?* Anirban wondered.

Campaigning ended with the president's debate. Polling was scheduled 48 hours later.

In the past three weeks, Anirban had felt like a taxi moving from one hostel to another, showing his face at public meetings like a starlet before her first release.

On the day of the election, he was asked to report to the voting centre early in the morning. 'You cannot ask for votes. That would be against the rules. But stand in front of the door near the booth from the start to the end of voting,' his campaign co-ordinator Biswal told him.

'Remember the last impression is the best impression,' he finished with a flourish.

Being a Free Thinker candidate in the Leftist bastion wasn't a pleasant experience even on the last day of elections for Anirban. Some students were downright rude: 'Don't irritate me, boss.' Others were melodramatic: 'Won't vote for the FT till the day I die.' A few were sarcastic, such as the student who said: 'Oye, Free Thinker, *tujhe main ek vote zaroor doonga*. But you have to show me that skit right now.' Everybody laughed.

He saw Geetha queuing up to vote around 4 p.m. He walked up to her. Before he could utter anything, she said, half in jest, 'Don't ask for my vote. You cannot be campaigning right now.'

Anirban smiled, 'I was just going to ask why you didn't turn up at 7 p.m. that day.'

She smiled back and said, 'There's a big, big reason.'

And then she told him, in hushed tones, that she had been very busy because last week a relationship that had been hanging fire for the past two years had finally fructified.

'It was an on-off kind of thing between Srinivas and me. But the other night, it all came together. It was a magical night, you know. Everything we wanted to tell each other but for some strange reason never had—it happened that night. He is going to Chicago for his doctorate next year. Hopefully, we will be married before that.'

Then she held his hand, like a nurse holding a patient's, with a mix of authority and tenderness. 'I hope I haven't hurt you in any way,' she said.

Wow! So there was something from your side as well, or you wouldn't have said something like this, Anirban thought.

'Where did you get that impression? We will always be friends,' he whispered, without meaning a single syllable.

'I was just being sure. See you later.'

'See you later.'

The counting began around 8 the same night at the Down Campus. It was carnival time. Not so much drinking as shouting slogans and dancing. Songs of revolution rose from the cadre in a passionate chorus. Decades of cultural activism by the faithful had created a library of lyrics dipped in fiery red. For all the anti-incumbency mood, the Commies were still confident of clinching the polls. As in the West Bengal state assembly elections, they seemed to have worked out the electoral arithmetic to the E.

Shivalkar walked away with over 500 votes, an eye-popping number for an NSUI candidate in JNU. Most would have been ecstatic to reach 50. The intelligent view was that Shivalkar would divide the anti-SFI vote, allowing Buddhadeb to sail through.

Much like pundits in national polls, they were wrong. Yogendra triumphed by 100-odd votes. The result wasn't *as* shocking as India winning the 1983 World Cup, but pretty unexpected all the same.

Yogendra was the only FT winner in the central panel. The SFI–AISF panel had claimed the remaining three seats. The Left duo had also retained a majority of seats for councillors. The shock loss of the prestigious president's post aside, JNU continued to be a Red fort.

In the first three rounds of counting, Anirban was very much in the race. The Bihari in a Bengali avatar looked like working in his favour. But in the last round, he lost steam and fell short by 10 votes. Everybody consoled him as if he had suffered a family bereavement.

Anirban's own feelings were mixed. He knew success would have raised his social profile. But he was also aware that it would have meant getting tied down by students' union meetings and demonstrations. He actually felt relieved that he wouldn't have to do any of that. It was a grand experience but, thank God, it was over. Isn't that what Sharad had told him?

When Anirban returned to the hostel early in the morning, he found Bhatia eating Maggi. 'I love Maggi,' he said. 'It is food's version of a 3 a.m. friend—warm and comforting.'

But he didn't show the faintest interest in finding out who had won or lost in the elections. Not even about his roommate. *That's what love does to you,* Anirban thought, *it shrinks your universe to a single person.*

And then it struck him like a thunderbolt: the stark contradiction in Geetha's avowed position. He remembered that the night after the introduction party when they had gone out for dinner at Ganga dhaba, she had told him, 'I like people who are involved in changing things around them.' Her ideal man was an idealist trying to change the world, she had said.

Now Anirban wondered if a Leftist going to Chicago for his PhD was idealism of any kind. But he decided not to be harsh with her. Because he had realized by now that, as human beings, we are not always able to live up to our own ideals. And it doesn't mean we were lying in the first place.

14

Nirula's

In the famous Saadat Hasan Manto short story, *Boo* (Odour), a man cannot forget the smell of a *ghatam,* a woman from the hills, he once makes love to during a rainy afternoon. The odour settles on his skin and seeps into his soul. And he looks for that unnameable, irresistible odour everywhere, including the body of his bride on their wedding night.

The JNU omelette had a similar odour with its own stamp of copyright. Ask anyone who has spent a couple of years in any of the hostels whether he or she can tell a JNU omelette from any other in the universe.

Students who had left the campus 10 years ago would suddenly find it in the unlikeliest of places: a restaurant in Shillong, a dhaba in Ludhiana or a tea stall in Kochi—and find themselves smiling at a half-remembered memory. The smell was unmistakeable, unforgettable.

For most students, JNU mornings began with the tea kept in a steel barrel outside the mess: hot, oversweet and unlimited. Sometimes Anirban would fill his glass, keep it on the study table and go back to bed. Like a spurned lover, the tea would turn cold in time. Over the next few days, houseflies would sip on it, some would get trapped and perish in their eagerness to taste the sweet liquid, turned swampy by now. The tea would ferment further, creating a ring of yellow scum that was near-impossible to wash off.

Anirban didn't care. Neither did Bhatia, who pretty much followed a similar style. Or even Svetlana, the permanent house guest. She always brought her large Russian mug which, unsurprisingly, had Vladimir Ilyich Lenin's name printed on it.

Lunch was strictly vegetarian. Those from the not-so-affluent families would enjoy the basic meal—kadhi-chawal, aloo-gobhi, dal-roti or something like that. The boys from well-off homes would crib every day. Andhra boys would get their gunpowder and mix it in the rice, hoping to find a taste of mother's kitchen. Those from Assam would bring bamboo-shoot pickle; others from the North-East would carry dried fish pickle, drawing disapproving scowls from the vegetarians.

Dinners were relatively classy affairs. Mutton, chicken and egg—all with the same version of curry—were served once a week. But those with more demanding taste buds would still complain. For them everything was bitter gourd. They wanted better meals, and discussed the special dinners of public schools: chicken roast and steamed ginger pudding. They would talk about family dinners in the Gymkhana Club. Some would go for a jaunt out of the campus for something more to their liking.

JNU rules ensured that class distinctions were underplayed in the campus. If you could rustle up Rs 200–300 for the mess bill and about Rs 20 per month for the hostel room, you could survive. Of course, it meant that you couldn't treat anybody to more than a nimboo-pani or a bun-omelette—which, anyway, was practically 80 per cent of the dhaba's menu. It was like living in a primitive society where wants and needs were restricted. In JNU, taste buds, too, were democratized for lack of options.

Dates were cheap. The costliest treat in the Up Campus came to less than Rs 2—Rs 1.80 to be precise—and the guy at the counter would always return the change. That was the cost of a bun-omelette in the Ganga dhaba. You could relax with a glass of nimboo-pani for Rs 1. Tea and coffee were cheaper. But it was tough to tell the difference between the two. At Down Campus, a gentleman named Francis served a heavenly mango shake.

Every item's price was regulated by the Commie-controlled student union, which believed that even a vegetable roll was fine dining. The dhabawala was a small-time capitalist, a petit bourgeois! How could he be allowed to fleece and loot the students?

The restrictions meant that money had little use in the campus. At Kamal Complex, a restaurant served tomato egg-drop soup for Rs 5 or so; by common consensus the worst in the world.

To pamper one's date, or celebrate with one's friends, one had to step outside the campus. Those who really loved spicy chicken done the tandoori way visited Sona Rupa, a small restaurant in Yusuf Sarai market near AIIMS. The DTC bus number 666 + took you there.

Students also went to Rajinder da Dhaba, the roadside eatery outside Kamal Cinema. Or, even to Chanakya Cinema where you feasted on momos in one of the faceless shops lined up near the Yashwant shopping complex. The complex was the preferred haunt of big mamas, prolific shoppers, from the USSR; some shops had their names written only in Russian. A couple of joints at Munirka which served south Indian food as well as vegetarian Chinese fare were relatively cheaper haunts. Students with cash juggled these options. The huts at the Essex Farm were a more exclusive option, especially for lovers who believed in value-for-money meals of a different kind.

But the real go-to place was the Nirula's at the Priya Cinema complex. The latter was a low-priced, single-screen theatre showing horror films of the Ramsay brothers and Mohan Bakhri. Rickshawalas and the area's vast underclass watched these movies, often putting their legs up on the seat in front. JNU students also went there; especially those from the small towns of Bihar and Uttar Pradesh seeking relief from the Film Club movies of Andre Wajda and Sergei Eisenstein, which horrified them in another way.

The local fast-food chain, Nirula's, was as much an eatery as an idea. It was a giant step that the unpolished small-town student took into the great culinary unknown. It opened up their taste buds to the tricky, even frightening world of pizzas, burgers and footlongs.

Taste buds are resistant creatures. There is a tussle,

sometimes bitter and lasting, to overcome the deeply held belief that there's no tastier food than what Mother cooks. Everything else is a compromise. A few of the small-towners would be overwhelmed by apprehensions never to return again. But most of them went ahead, conquering their fears because they knew that to be comfortable meant you were in the process of scrubbing off some of that small-town stink those dainty girls from south Delhi found so revolting.

Taking a girl to Nirula's generally meant you were either serious about her or luring her for some late-night love. The Commies abhorred Nirula's. At least, that was their public posture. To them, it represented a form of bourgeois indulgence and those who visited the place were labelled as the 'enemy of the people'. It was as if the food chain was a totem of capitalist evil.

It is another matter that one Leftie leader was often spotted at this den of culinary vice. In fact, his visits were so frequent that one of the political parties came out with a pamphlet against him, titled *Pizza Communism*.

Shamefaced, and allegedly being nudged by other party leaders, he stopped going to Nirula's. The rumour, though, was that he could now be spotted at the more expensive but far more distant United Coffee House in Connaught Place.

Anirban's first visit to Nirula's happened immediately after the polls. He was walking towards the mess room for another unappetizing dinner when he heard Robi call out for him. 'Where are you going?' he wanted to know.

'To the mess. Where else?' he replied.

'Come with us,' Jack said, who was walking with Robi. 'We are going to eat out to celebrate Yogendra' victory.'

Yogendra smiled and nodded. For some reason, Jack's girlfriend was missing. *Have they fallen out?* Anirban couldn't help thinking.

Soon they were walking beyond Kamal Complex, past the cluster of giant rocks, along a narrow man-made trail. Anirban marvelled how such pathways were always the shortest and the simplest. He had observed the phenomena in the Garhwal hills and could see the same here as they moved alongside the undergrowth. Couples were already settling down behind the rocks, much like in Marine Drive. As the night progressed, some would go back to the hostels. Others would emerge only a few hours before the sun rose.

'Isn't that Monali of the Japanese centre?' Jack asked no one in particular. He was looking at a girl sitting at some distance.

'Looks like it,' Robi said. '*Isi liye kehte hain ki bhoot aur choot kahin bhi mil sakte hain*—you can find ghosts and pussy anywhere!'

Robi's insightful remark had them all laughing uproariously.

Now they had crossed the Grade IV staff quarters and had come to a boundary wall that had to be scaled. Somebody had helpfully piled up a bunch of bricks hugging the wall. One by one they crossed over; Anirban, the leanest but also the least athletic of the group, being the last.

Another 50 yards and they arrived at a tri-junction. The

road on the left led to Vasant Kunj, an upcoming colony of the influential middle-class. The road on the right led to the Munirka flats and a DTC bus depot.

But they walked straight towards Hotel Vasant Continental. 'Are we going to Nirula's?' He had heard that the fast-food restaurant was somewhere in the vicinity.

'What do you think?' Robi smiled indulgently.

Nirula's immediately put Anirban in a good mood. A sexy red colour dominated the interiors. Whatever your age, you felt young and wanted inside. The ice creams with exotic names such as Manhattan Mania, Rum Raisin and 21 Love reminded him of American teen comics. He noticed Ms Niharika, the porcelain beauty of his batch, sitting with Alistair Fulcrum, a visiting Marxist scholar from Cambridge.

Whipsmart and with-it, Niharika had openly announced having Chicago on her mind. She had an attractive drawl that seemed to exude part boredom, part bedroom. Her nose was always high, just like her heels.

Alistair was working on his PhD on the intellectual history of nineteenth-century Bengal. The manner in which they were talking to each other suggested they might have found the fulcrum of each other's life. Niharika caught Anirban staring at them but decided to look through him. Anirban felt reproached and began concentrating on the menu.

He had been to several restaurants in Ranchi. They didn't serve pizzas and footlongs but offered quality continental food of a different kind. For a moment, his mind wandered back to the Chinese restaurants of his childhood. Chung Wa near the overbridge and Sutlor right opposite the British Council Library. Then there was Waldorf, a very old restaurant near Welfare Cinema. The chicken chowmein at Hong Kong, near the 'kutchery', was part of his indelible epicurean memory.

The food at these family-oriented eateries had a distinctive smell of ajino-moto and soya sauce that in time had become his reference point for Chinese gastronomy. Whenever and wherever he went to a Chinese restaurant, he would search for that smell.

Anirban didn't know what to order. Not wanting to appear ignorant and confused, he asked for a salami footlong with extra toppings of mushroom and tomato. Both Robi and Jack opted for the chicken pot pie. Anirban carefully stored the name in a corner of his mind for future reference.

Having placed the order, Robi asked Anirban to watch out for the number on the board. The number on the LED indicator was 177. They had to wait till 183. Anirban enjoyed watching people proceed to the counter with a bounce in their step as their number flashed with the sign: Your order is ready.

'Isn't that Niharika Kapoor with that Brit?' Robi was nudging him. Anirban just nodded his head.

'*Yeh bhi gayee lagta hai*,' said Jack and looked meaningfully at Robi. The two broke into a typical guffaw that men often burst into after sharing a joke with a sexual innuendo. Yogendra seemed to be smiling only under peer pressure.

Anirban didn't like the crassness of that laughter. He knew by now that Jack was no different from hundreds of other north Indian students in the campus who could be pretty liberal in their political and personal life on one hand, and yet pretty judgemental about women on the other.

In JNU, only a minuscule section of students believed that anything worth doing could be done openly. The dominant view on sex was essentially small-town and patriarchal.

JNU was politically progressive—but socially conservative at its core.

There was a campus code for love, especially among those denied its pleasures. The frusto lot would bunch girls primarily into two categories: *deti hai* (one who sleeps around) and *nahi deti hai* (one who doesn't sleep around). There was a third category, too: *sahlane deti hai par ghusane nahi* (one who allows you to feel her up but not fuck her). Girls who did not have sexual intercourse (even with their boyfriends), or at least appeared not to, were highly respected among the overtly conservative.

All the guys were thoroughly conflicted on women and sex. Many of them had great clarity in their political ideas but were thoroughly confused in matters of women and relationships.

They enjoyed the openness of an urban situation that allowed them to date and mate. A few would even have a relationship with a girl, hiding the fact that they were married. Even those seriously involved with a girl would admit in private that they preferred to marry a traditional girl of their parents' choice back home. This was for two reasons. Dowry, of course, was one of them. But, more importantly, they were never confident about handling an independent woman. A rich, attractive, educated but dependent wife is what they wanted and, most often, what they got, if they landed a job that was valued in the dowry bazaar. This was the hypocrisy and schizophrenia that small-town India bred.

It was tough for a girl whose sexual fling was cracked wide open in public. A student discovered this to her dismay after an African student she had slept with, gleefully recounted the night in detail to his hostel friends. Soon, the story spread like bushfire. Made to feel like a slut, she withdrew into a shell.

Yet for most girls, JNU was close to heaven. For all its limitations, the place was still a haven compared to the small-town prisons many of them came from.

No. 183 flashed on the digital electronic screen.

Anirban fetched the order but discovered that the footlong looked orphaned. There was no salami on it. He pointed out the mistake to Yogendra, who immediately strode to the counter. The issue was quickly settled with the manager asking his staff to replace the footlong with a fresh one.

Then he let fall a parting shot, 'Sorry, sir. I am happy it is all settled now. You know the guy who took the order is a Bihari. You can understand why all this must have happened.'

The manager was about to turn away when Jack jumped out of his chair and held him by the collar. 'What do you mean by saying he is a Bihari?' Jack growled. He was shaking in anger.

The manager was too shocked to react. Eventually he blubbered, 'Why are you getting angry, sir? I didn't say anything to you.'

He didn't seem to comprehend the damage he had done. For many in Delhi, it was normal to use the word 'Bihari' pejoratively to describe migrants from the eastern state. The word was a not-so-subtle sneer.

'Do you know I am also a Bihari?' Jack was on the point of slapping him. Yogendra was desperately trying to calm him down and Robi was simply shell-shocked by the sudden turn of events.

'How can you be a Bihari, sir? You are educated,' the manager stammered in reply.

Then the penny dropped for Jack. It was beyond the manager's comprehension that the smart young man holding his collar could also be a Bihari. A smelly, uncouth, tobacco-chewing dim-witted rickshawala or a daily wager—that's how the average middle-class Dilliwala typified Bihar. He certainly didn't have the faintest idea that Bihar also produced hundreds of civil servants and IITians every year.

Before he could say anything more, the manager started blabbering loudly, 'I am so sorry, sir, so sorry. I apologize…I apologize.'

Jack let him go and settled back on his chair after

Yogendra said, '*Jaane do yaar, mitti daalo*…Let it go, man.' They had their meal quietly. The unpleasant incident had left a bad taste in the mouth. That, however, did not stop Anirban from enjoying the six slices of salami served with mozzarella cheese on his footlong.

He couldn't help thinking about the importance of regional identity and how it could make someone so aggressive. Anirban knew very well that back in Bihar, nobody was a Bihari. Out there, everyone was identified by his or her caste. That part was cast in stone.

In central Bihar, where Anirban had spent his childhood, he was always identified as a Bengali. He was often taunted with abuses such as *Bangaali poncha, baap ka daahdi nocha* (Stinking Bengali pulls his father's beard).

The abuse didn't make any sense. It was just meant to irritate him. And it did. However, it also firmed up his self-identity as a Bengali. But as he grew up, he realized that he found himself gelling far more easily with Biharis than Bengalis. Barring the language he spoke with his parents and the food he ate at home, he was a Bihari to the marrow—from his accent to the abuses he flung about.

It is funny, he thought, *how old identities have a way of emerging in our lives.* He wouldn't have thought that Jack, who came from small-town Samastipur in north-central Bihar but had grown up studying in public schools all over India, would react in that fashion.

He felt quite proud of the way Yogendra and Jack had stood up for themselves. As they got up to leave, the manager once again came up and said sorry. He also offered them free ice cream, which they politely refused. As all four were walking out of the door, Anirban decided to take one last look at Niharika. She was staring at them. Maybe she wasn't so oblivious to her surroundings after all.

The next morning, the brawl found its way to a SFI pamphlet against Yogendra, Jack and Robi. Being too lowly in the ranking, Anirban had been spared. The headline declared: *JNUSU's FT President in fistfight at Nirula's*. The pamphlet brought out by the SFI condemned him for indulging in violence. The cleverly worded lines described Yogendra and Jack getting into a highly avoidable fight with an employee of Nirula's. It was expressly written to make them appear as the instigators of the row. The pamphlet also made the point that only the SFI was committed to discipline and peace on the campus.

When fellow hostellers came to know that Anirban was also present at the scene of crime, they prodded him for juicier details. Anirban gave out his version. Some believed him. But many, especially the SFI sympathizers, didn't. Truth, as the great Japanese filmmaker Akira Kurosawa showed in *Rashomon*, isn't always what you see or hear but what you want to see or hear.

15

The culture

ANIRBAN HATED TERM papers. They were like fortnightly rashes that left him itchy and irritated. He was forced to analyse a bunch of articles he didn't even want to read. Then one had to distill them into an academically acceptable argument in 1,500 words, which again, he didn't really believe in. Of course, this had to be followed by a discussion where the gentleman or the lady on the other side of the table drilled cavernous holes in them. This wasn't his idea of studying history; especially when he was aware that his goal was the civil services, not a seat in SOAS.

But this term paper had excited Anirban like none other. For the first time, he had found a topic he really wanted to work on: *Tamas* and the Communal Problem. *Tamas*, a teleserial made by Govind Nihalani based on the famous Partition novel by Bhisham Sahni and shown on DD, had created a huge controversy. This was history and literature at a crucial intersection. For once, the professor was in agreement with him and gave the nod for a term paper. That's what got him considerably charged.

Anirban was halfway through the paper when he felt his concentration sagging. *How about the hair cut that I have been putting off since last month?* he asked himself. He checked his wallet and found it staring blankly back at him. He cursed himself for not having withdrawn Rs 50 the day before and ambled over to the bank.

Poised in front of the Godavari girls' hostel, the bank was the size of a large hut but built, rather needlessly, like a fortress. Even if it was the last depository of cash on earth, no self-respecting robber would have attempted a heist. Who would rob a bank where students routinely took out as little as Rs 10, where the collective transaction was as high as Rs 5000 per day? Anirban pocketed the entire Rs 170 scholarship that the central government lavished on merit-cum-means students like him every month. Feeling like a millionaire, he started walking towards Kamal Complex.

A Leftie rally in support of the Palestine cause was en route. Anirban loved looking at the faces of marchers during a demonstration. To him, every demo was a case study in leadership and hierarchy. As usual, the leaders were in the front. And as usual, the placards were being carried by a couple of attractive cadres freshly drafted into Communism with stardust in their eyes. Intense and solemn, the leaders walked behind them, seemingly burdened by the weight of the world.

The real action heroes and heroines of the show were the lead slogan-shouters, and quite a few of them were women. Anirban saw Geetha Kasturi among them.

Like the others, she was screaming at the top of her lungs; her veins filled with blood and passion ready to burst out of their secret core. *Imperialism Down, Down!,* she shouted followed by *SFI, March On!.* The cadres were echoing in unison: *March on, March on.* Anirban recalled someone telling him, sarcastically, that if all the *March on*s of JNU were written down on a roll of paper, it would probably stretch to Moscow and back.

Staying behind the protesters and wondering if Geetha had spotted him or not, Anirban resumed his brief journey to Kamal Complex. Located on the other side of the Sutlej hostel, the Kamal Complex was the great shopping experience of JNU. There was a bookstore, a barber's, a tailor's, a general store and a restaurant that generally molested the cuisine it served. What more did civilization need?

At the casual but erudite bookstore, Anirban found Sharad flipping through a volume of verse by Muktibodh, the Hindi poet who died unrewarded in his lifetime and was regarded as a genius now.

Sharad asked Anirban, 'Do you know the gentleman sitting there owns this Geeta Book Centre?'

Anirban looked towards the direction Sharad was pointing at with his eyes and saw a middle-aged gentleman who looked somewhat like Engels. He shook his head.

'Everybody calls him Dada. It is men like him who have made JNU what it is. This small bookstore probably has the highest per-inch space for books on Marxism, the entire Left canon. But he has got much more stuff. If you are looking for any book on semiotics, post-modernism, post-structuralism, Dada is likely to get it for you. Jacques Derrida, Michele Foucault, Roland Barthes—he is actually one of those booksellers who would have probably read many of the books he sells. He is a real bookstore owner, not one of those fake ones in Khan Market. See, there are also books on Hindi poetry and literary criticism. You can buy the poetry of Nagarjun or Kedarnath Singh or read Namwar Singh's literary criticism. Dada is one of JNU's landmarks,' Sharad said.

They were heading towards Ganga dhaba now. 'Till the last couple of years, the Nilgiri dhaba was a hotter nightspot than the Ganga dhaba. Now it has overshadowed Nilgiri by a mile. Even a recent suicide by one of the Ganga dhaba owners has done nothing to bring down its popularity,' Sharad said.

'What are you guys doing here?' Anirban heard a voice.

He turned around to see someone shaking hands with Sharad. 'I am Shubhalok,' he introduced himself to Anirban and sat down.

'He is working on his PhD on Beckett,' Sharad offered.

'For the past six years now. I am a JNU artefact,' he said self-deprecatingly. He was right. Shubhalok had a beard and was smoking a 501 beedi, two attributes that immediately certified anybody as a bonafide campus intellectual.

'We were discussing how Ganga dhaba has suddenly become so popular,' Sharad said.

'You never know with these places. Maybe 20 years

down the line, it will be looked at as JNU heritage property, a sort of cultural institution. See, the dhaba has no character. It has no distinctiveness either. But I like this place. I like boys and girls chatting deep into the night over anything and everything under the sun. There is always something meaningful in debates without a specific agenda. You enrich yourself with life's take-aways, things that enable you to negotiate life.'

They chatted for some time on Maradona (to which Anirban contributed) and Ben Okri (to which Anirban contributed by nodding vigorously most of the time). Shubhalok appeared to know a lot about African writers in general and Okri in particular, though Anirban wasn't the best person to evaluate him on the subject.

They were about to leave when Sharad suddenly asked Shubhalok, 'Has anyone ever told you that you have overstayed in the campus?'

It was a pretty rude question. But Shubhalok didn't seem to mind at all. On the contrary, his eyes lit up like Jack's, when offered a chance to pontificate.

'I came to JNU in 1980 for my Master's. And like some others, I am witness to two eras—the pre-1983 JNU and the post-1983 JNU. For most students today, names like Rajan James, Probir Purkayastha, Jalees Ahmed, Nalini Ranjan Mohanty—would mean little. But for our generation, and those of the earlier years, they are markers of unforgettable events, and reminders of how the campus changed and why.

'Many of my classmates are gone. But the truth is

nobody pesters you on that account. Few people make you feel like a relic. JNU is not judgemental. That's its greatest strength. JNU doesn't like ambition or attitude, but adores adda. For me, and there are many like me, the place is an addiction. There is no premium on success. And the word 'loser' does not exist. So many students are jobless and frustrated. But how many suicides do you hear of?'

'See, there are four kinds of students here,' he continued. 'A small number make it to the civil services or to the world of American or European academia—the two most sought-after medals for an arts student conforming to social norms. The Calcutta students are masters at winning foreign scholarships. They know how, when and where to apply. It is like a relay race run from one generation after another. By the way, have you seen how so many Bongs from Presidency College appear to be in transit?

'There is another tier of students who end up getting jobs in state civil services in Rajasthan or Madhya Pradesh or Bihar, in banks as probationary officers or in LIC as assistant administrative officers. Some also become lecturers in places like Shillong, Gwalior, Jaisalmer and Sagar. Often these jobs mean going to back-of-the-beyond places, boondocks where company is the biggest problem, especially for those who are prone to constipation without a late-night discussion on Heidegger or Habermas.

'Yet many jump at these offers. Opportunities are extremely limited. There is a time in everyone's career when any job is a good job. Going to these far-off places also has its perks. It is life without any kind of pressure:

an anonymous but pretty respectable existence. It's not exactly why one had come to JNU in the first place. The truth is: Life isn't always what we want but what we get.

'But there is another category of students. Those working on their PhDs for the sixth year or worse, like me. We are actually unemployed. Some of us don't want to work for the government. That would be too statist. Others refuse even to entertain the possibility of doing a job because it goes against their self-image. They are prisoners of false pride. They dream of Cambridge or Chicago but aren't good enough to be there and too vain to accept the truth.

'Just a handful are rebels against the system by choice, men who want to change the world. There are frauds among them too; phoneys feeding off their girlfriends' money. After all, revolution costs money. And generally it is the girlfriends' money.'

His explanation was long but it didn't seem like a monologue to Anirban.

'I totally agree,' Sharad said, 'I have been here for only a few months but I understand what you mean. JNU gets into your guts. But I see many positives too.

'JNU makes you aware and alive. It gives you a looking glass to the world. But like a prism, it also colours your world-view. At the end of it all, though, I think there's something that distinguishes JNU from other universities in our country. JNU is that rare place from where you emerge with a conscience. You learn that there are causes, which may not have anything to do with your career, but are worth fighting and dying for. It doesn't matter that only a few actually work for that goal. It is important that everyone becomes aware of such a possibility.

'In a sense, JNU is in the business of making citizens out of boys and girls. And it isn't only because of what is taught in the class but what you learn from seniors, hostellers and classmates. Boys and girls arrive carrying suitcases packed with past and prejudice. JNU upends and recasts you as a socially aware individual. You come to know who and what you are—and why.'

'Do you know what educated me in JNU?' Shubhalok asked.

'What?' Both Sharad and Anirban were curious.

'The pamphlets,' he replied. 'For me,' Shubhalok continued, 'pamphlets are fundamental to JNU's political conversation.'

The pamphlets were like free pickles that spiced up JNU meals and, in a sense, made them unique. A pamphlet could be spun around anything or everything that a political party felt was worth going public with. Occasionally, an independent group or even an individual would spell out his views on a hostel episode, a national occurrence or even an international event. Some passionate pieces penned by campus mavericks and dissidents were far more readable than the drab stuff churned out by the parties.

The pamphlets were cyclostyled on A/4 sheets of coarse paper, about 100-odd kept by the mess counter of every hostel, imploring for eyeballs during breakfast, lunch or dinner. You picked them up on the way to the table.

Some would ignore them. These were generally the UPSC types. For them, the mess was an avenue of de-stressing and unwinding. These guys would mark their schedules to the last second like Korean executives: 15 minutes for lunch, 10 minutes in the common room, five minutes at the cigarette shop, two minutes in the loo. When time was money, how could one waste it on something as mundane as a pamphlet?

Others would grab a pamphlet out of sheer habit and place it next to their plates and wouldn't even spare a glance after that. Some would read a few lines and then blasphemically spill their dal over the sheet. A few would chew on and digest every word of what was written along with the rice and the bhindi ki sabji. Some would sit alongside like-minded guys and discuss the subject of the day, sometimes past the mess hours.

Shubhalok was probably one of them.

At the end, the mess floor would be peppered with pamphlets stained yellow with curry like a stadium strewn with leftovers after a rock concert. Perhaps those pamphlets were JNU's core, its soul in disposable black and white.

When Anirban returned to his room, he saw a new message on the same door across his room: 'I am horny, I am stoned. I am drenched to the bone.' *This isn't the language of a pamphlet writer*, he told himself.

16

DTC

THE MONTHLY DELHI Transport Corporation (DTC) bus pass was every student's unlikely lifeline. The pass cost Rs 12.50 per month and allowed unlimited access to the city. It allowed you to feast on the finest art movies at Shakuntalam, get depressed watching the experimental plays at NSD, took you to Chandni Chowk for Ved Prakash's lemon soda. And if someone was kind enough to offer a key to an MIG flat in Dilshad Garden, find some sweaty afternoon sex with an enterprising girlfriend.

For everybody, barring UGC scholarship holders who could afford the expensive autos and the odd guy who had a motorbike, it was the only mode of transport. It was painful waiting for the bus, especially in the summer afternoons when the frequency dipped while temperatures rose. Rather unwittingly, DTC played a critical role in fashioning the JNU ethos. Buses democratized travel, fostered familiarity. It created an egalitarian travel culture. Everybody knew everybody. DTC ensured JNU remained an urban village.

Even the unadventurous bookworm knew at least three

DTC bus routes by heart: 666, 666 + and 615. 666 took you from Poorvanchal to Down Campus, where the SIS and SL were housed; 666 + followed the same route but went beyond Down Campus. It turned left to Munirka before swerving right towards RK Puram and the five-star Hyatt hotel. Then it pushed through the Ring Road till it arrived at AIIMS where it took another right turn, sailed past Uphaar Cinema, Aurobindo Place and reached IIT. From there, it was back to Down Campus and Poorvanchal hostel.

615 was every student's hotline to the city. Munirka, Safdarjang Enclave, Netaji Nagar (this is where you got off if you were going to Chanakya, the hottest theatre in town), Sarojini Nagar (a stunning combo of the most with-it and the most affordable clothes for the fashionably young), Prithviraj Road, National Archives (unavoidable for the senior history student), Le Meredien, Janpath, Connaught Place and Minto Road railway station.

The DTC buses were the city's vertebrae. The yellow and green buses kept Delhi on the move. In a city of two long summers—first, the dry, pre-monsoon heat and then the post-monsoon version typified by a killer humidity—the bus rides often wrenched something vital out of you. When you emerged from the ride, you were broken, beaten, a lesser person than when you stepped in 45 minutes earlier. Every journey was a body-bruising, soul-crushing ordeal.

Whenever anybody vacated a seat, more than one person would rush to replace him. There would always be a smugly triumphant winner and a shame-faced loser.

Occasionally, a gentleman would invite a 'ladies' to sit alongside him. Some refused the offer; others didn't. Sharing the seat meant rubbing shoulders with a stranger. Literally. Many abhorred that.

To strangers in the city, a bus ride evoked a sense of fear. Delhi had recovered from the physical scars of the anti-Sikh riots of 1984 when marauding mobs led by Congress leaders had turned the city in to an open air abattoir where Sikhs were slashed, hacked and burnt.

But some time ago, Khalistani extremists had carried out a series of transistor bomb blasts in the buses. Anirban had been warned by friends to be careful inside a DTC bus. For the first few months, whenever he travelled by bus outside the campus, he would feel a little nervous.

It didn't help that a terse message was block-printed at the back of every seat: *1. Look Below Your Seat 2. There Could Be A Bomb 3. Raise Alarm 4. Earn Reward.*

But as he spent more time in Delhi, like everyone else, Anirban became inured to the message, its banality. In any case, there was no other way to travel. Who could stop commuting for something as inevitable as death?

Every day, a fleet of DTC buses swallowed and vomited people and fumes across the city. People lived an entire life around a single bus number: 327 from Mayur Vihar Phase I to Central Secretariat (Kendriya Sachivalaya, actually), 680 Malviya Nagar to C-Sec, 851 from Uttam Nagar to ITO (the income tax office). The bus picked them up every morning and dropped them to a pointless office for a day without beauty or ambition and then took them back home for a night of loveless sex.

Always swollen with commuters, DTC buses were a sex-starved male's paradise too. In this cauldron of lesser people, riddled with unending anxieties and failed aspirations, aggression came out in the ugliest of ways. Shape, age, size, looks—nothing mattered. For some pricks, any and every woman was a potential target for anything—rubbing, touching, fondling, pinching, squeezing and everything else that could be possibly done in a bus meant to carry 60 and possibly ferrying 120. The sarkari babus smelling of sweat, Pan Parag and the cheapest perfumes that bribes could buy, their paunches bursting out of their pants with an unbearable horniness, crammed the buses. They were the worst offenders, girls told Anirban.

You could easily spot a hunter on the bus. He would snuggle up to a woman and get within rubbing and touching distance. Some women would squirm uncomfortably and try to move away—which was about two inches in that sardine-like situation. He would then inch closer, look elsewhere while gently rubbing himself against her. A few would glare at him. But only the rarest of rare woman would holler at him, with a fierce *'Apne ang apne paas rakh!'* Then the offender would react with injured innocence at being told to keep his body parts to himself. But on most days, a hunter would have his day. For it wasn't easy for a woman to speak out and receive empathy and support in a male-dominated bus that, ideologically, was almost like a khap on wheels.

As a normal, sex-starved 21-year-old post-graduate student, Anirban was always conflicted while travelling in a bus. Sometimes, watching others do it, he would get this wild desire to grab the limp breasts of some forgettable 40-plus woman standing next to him. In his mind, he would construct an entire episode of fast and furious love. These highly pleasant reveries would considerably reduce the agony of standing in a crowded bus for 45 minutes or more; the journey would get over in a jiffy, invariably leaving him with a half-smile and a full erection.

But he always resisted the urge to grab. Some half-remembered moral science lesson by one of the Jesuit brothers in school or something his mother may have told him while serving lunch would stop him from doing what he felt like doing. He just couldn't force himself on unwilling women. Even in his fantasies the women were always willing.

But what happened that day wasn't fantasy. Anirban took the bus from Patel Nagar after appearing in a test for Allahabad Bank Probationary Officers. His heart wasn't really in it. But fear makes you do all kinds of things. One morning at the mess table, he was asked, 'What will you do, if the civil services option doesn't work out? This is a great back-up.' Anirban had filled up the form. Now he was going back after the test with one thought firmly ensconced in his head—*Aptitude tests are not for me.*

These tests were held on Sunday. Somewhere around Moti Bagh, a young girl got into the bus. In her grey salwar-kurta, she was more Meena Kumari than Mamta Kulkarni. She looked around—as if trying to sift the ruffians from the *bhalo chhele*s (the Bengali term for decent, well-behaved boys). Then she slowly moved towards Anirban, her intuition having plucked him out as one of the guys who wouldn't misbehave.

A bunch of rogues eyeing her almost audibly groaned in disappointment. Then, a couple of them started shifting towards the girl, who had taken shelter behind Anirban. The two men, both in their early 40s, wanted to stand next to the girl but Anirban was blocking the way.

One of them came within whispering distance of Anirban and said, *'Tu satana chahta hai, ya main laga doon?'* Anirban could hardly believe that the man was asking him to decide who should rub himself against the girl. It was like one of those questions that Anirban had faced in the aptitude test where you must choose and answer: a or b. Or both. There is generally a fourth choice too—none of the above. But Anirban wasn't given that choice here.

For an indecisive moment he looked back—the girl had instinctively fathomed what the other guys were up to. She looked at Anirban imploringly, like a lamb on the way to the slaughterhouse, hoping that she might be rescued by a stranger.

Suddenly, Anirban felt the unbearable, crushing tension of responsibility. And he discovered a sliver of courage that he didn't know existed in him. He could literally feel something rise in his heart and make its way to his throat. He said, *'Aap us taraf raho,'* sternly telling the rogues to stay away.

The hunter was taken aback at this unexpected resistance. He looked at his friend as if pondering the next course of action. Perhaps they thought this wasn't the right time to pick up a fight with someone who looked like a university student. They slunk away as most bullies do when confronted.

When the girl got down a few stops later, she just looked up at Anirban in a way that said, 'Thanks for being an angel.'

It was the best feeling he had had in a long, long time.

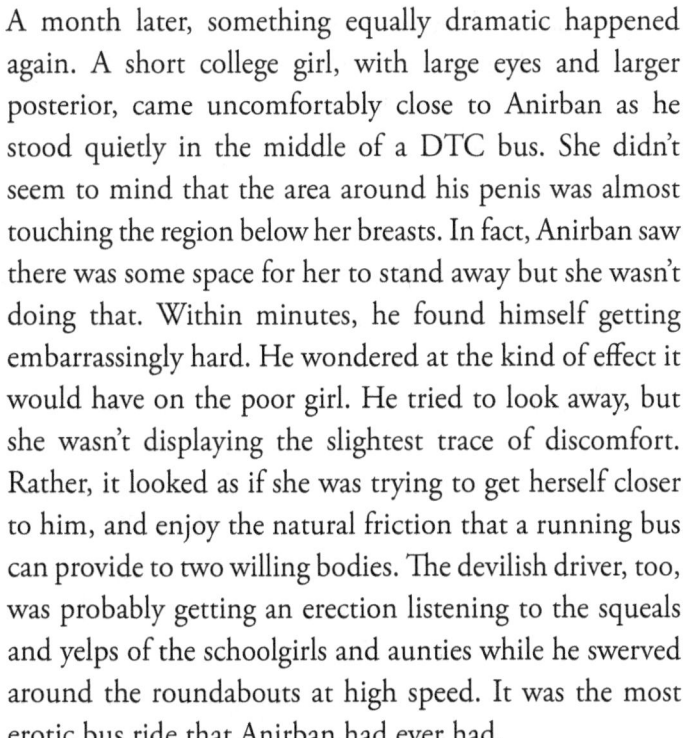

A month later, something equally dramatic happened again. A short college girl, with large eyes and larger posterior, came uncomfortably close to Anirban as he stood quietly in the middle of a DTC bus. She didn't seem to mind that the area around his penis was almost touching the region below her breasts. In fact, Anirban saw there was some space for her to stand away but she wasn't doing that. Within minutes, he found himself getting embarrassingly hard. He wondered at the kind of effect it would have on the poor girl. He tried to look away, but she wasn't displaying the slightest trace of discomfort. Rather, it looked as if she was trying to get herself closer to him, and enjoy the natural friction that a running bus can provide to two willing bodies. The devilish driver, too, was probably getting an erection listening to the squeals and yelps of the schoolgirls and aunties while he swerved around the roundabouts at high speed. It was the most erotic bus ride that Anirban had ever had.

The girl finally moved away from him as the driver

changed gears and the bus gathered speed after the Sarojini Nagar bus depot. She got down at the next stop, Netaji Nagar, in south Delhi.

Suddenly, Anirban became a helpless slave of his senses. He forgot he was due for a term paper the next day, comparing Dutch colonialism in Indonesia with British colonialism in India. He forgot he could be late for the special Wednesday meal when they served fiery chicken curry that had him salivating before dinner, and burning down below the morning after.

He, too, got off the bus at Netaji Nagar. She was walking slowly towards a narrow lane that branched off from the main road. Anirban hurried past her, took a lead of about 50 yards and stood quietly below a lamp post. A couple of scooters and a white Maruti car went by. There was nobody else but the two of them on the road. Anirban didn't know what to say, but he knew this much—something intense and physical had happened between them and it was mutual.

He had no idea why he was standing there and what he was going to say if the girl smiled at him and said hello. He was just a bundle of desire. He looked at the girl carefully as she took small steps towards him. With every step, Anirban found the feeling of desire being replaced with fear. What if the girl suddenly screamed? Suddenly, he wanted to run, or simply vanish for a few seconds till she passed by. But in that moment of reckoning, he just stood there frozen, looking away.

The girl had come very close by then. With the last

drop of courage left in his body, Anirban threw a sideways glance to see if she was looking at him or not. She wasn't. In fact, she was probably deliberately looking the other way to avoid eye contact.

Like him, perhaps, she had enjoyed something as a passing pleasure in the shadow of anonymity. But she wasn't interested in taking it forward. Anirban kept looking at her as she walked to a T-point another 50 yards ahead. Before she took the right turn, she stopped and looked back for a second as if trying to find out whether the guy had left or not.

Maybe she was scared too. Like Anirban, she too had surrendered to an instinct and was regretting it, apprehensive that she had done it with a potential stalker. In the next 30 seconds or so, she vanished from Anirban's sight into one of those grim flats that house a slice of sarkari Delhi, the homes of thousands of anonymous, faceless central government employees—men and women who await their annual dearness allowances as eagerly as greedy children for candies.

And as he sat at the bus stop waiting for the next 615, Anirban realized the true meaning of the phrase that he had first heard as a teenager in Bihar: KLPD—*Khare Lund Pe Dhokha*. The unforgettable description of a missed sexual opportunity, an erection cheated of its urgent purpose.

17

Going home

WHEN SUMMER ARRIVED, Anirban decided to go home. The first two semesters had flashed by faster than he had expected.

It felt as if only weeks before he had hobbled into that train to Delhi. A couple of friends had seen him off. 'Fuck Delhi,' or something like that, one of his friends had said. He remembered buying a copy of *Sportsworld* from the railway book stall to read on the way.

He had been upbeat and positive then. Now, he was an inventory of disappointments.

He wasn't proud of his academic achievements, which were actually totally lacking. Nothing had gone according to plan. To be more honest, he had done nothing according to plan. His grades were below par and, in spite of his unwillingness, he had contested the election. The only good thing was that he had lost. But now his self-esteem was as high as his shoelaces.

There was another reason why Anirban couldn't concentrate on course work. In his heart, he knew it was just a means towards an end. He wasn't able to follow what Sharad had asked him to do: 'Get a good Master's degree before you even start thinking of the civil services.' It depressed him to think about the wasted time.

A visit home, he thought, would make him feel better, give him a chance to clear his mind. *It will put me back in touch with reality*, he told himself.

When Anirban opened the rusty iron gate and stepped in, he saw his father working at the back in the kitchen garden. 'We grow our own vegetables,' he said rather proudly as Anirban bowed to touch his feet. He looked overjoyed at seeing him, but Anirban could see his eyes were sad.

'Why don't you write letters?' Ma complained.

Many students filed letters with the regularity of an official weekly despatch back home. The more organized blokes set aside a time for letter-writing. It was duty. But also a release of sorts, a way of connecting.

Anirban was disorganized about life in general. He sent postcards home once a month after receiving his money order. They were as brief as telegrams and read more like information bulletins. *Received money. I am all right and working hard. Hope you are keeping well. Regards.* His father sent him Rs 500 every month around the fifth after he had received his pension. He would wait, along with other students, for the postman by the hostel gate. That was all a letter from home meant to him.

'I have been busy,' he replied meekly. He didn't have

the courage to tell them both that he had contested the students' union elections. After washing his face, Anirban sat down for lunch.

'We have been growing potatoes and brinjal in the back garden,' his mother announced. 'Even spinach. Your father has been working hard.'

'Working hard? Hardly! What do you do with so much free time?' he said, rather embarrassed at the praise.

It was obvious he was growing vegetables not because he actually wanted to but because he had to. His parents needed to save every extra rupee for his higher education. Anirban felt ashamed of himself, for wasting time in campus politics and the lack of willpower to stick to his plan.

In the evening, he set out to meet his friends. They were happy to see him although they made fun of the Delhi lingo that had crept into his vocabulary. 'So how's JNU? Tell us about the girls. Have you humped any of them yet?' That was the normal opening line of most conversations.

They had all come to know about him dabbling in elections and scolded him for being so irresponsible. Anirban heard them out quietly. He knew they meant well. That's what small-town friendships are all about: life-long loyalty. With such friends, you could leave a conversation unfinished in a teashop, take off for the US, come back after 10 years and resume it without any fuss.

Anirban also realized that he no longer possessed their indifference. They were all stuck in time and were neither willing nor able to haul themselves out of the rut. They seemed resigned, probably were even content, to end up as shopkeepers and clerks and get married to undemanding girls who brought a decent dowry, produced kids and were happy to watch films like *Maang Bharo Sajna*.

Anirban didn't want any of that. In just one year, he had changed fundamentally. Inside.

At night, he sat down with his parents to watch the latest episode of *Circus* on Doordarshan. He liked the energy of the serial's young hero although his father found him to be 'upstartish'. As loadshedding struck, a loud grunt of disappointment rippled through the mohalla. 'You can hardly watch TV these days. Sometimes there is no electricity and sometimes the voltage is so low, you cannot even read a newspaper. It is terrible,' Ma said. It wasn't a complaint; more like the resigned response to an everyday occurrence by an ordinary person.

His parents looked like older versions of themselves. They appeared to have aged rapidly in the past one year. They spoke with an air of defeatedness, as though looking into a vista of dark days ahead. He was supposed to be the light at the end of the tunnel. What a joke that was turning out to be!

Anirban had come home on a month-long vacation. But after just a week, he asked during breakfast, whether he could leave in the next few days. He wasn't actually seeking permission, rather, he was announcing his decision.

He couldn't see his father's reaction. The light wasn't bright enough—and he didn't say anything.

His mother immediately exclaimed, '*O ma, ae kee!*' in

Bengali, which roughly meant, 'Why?' He tried to explain that the course work was demanding—and that he had to start preparing for the civil services. 'You can stay for at least a couple of weeks more,' she pleaded. But she went quiet when Baba said that Anirban was doing the right thing.

Next morning, he bought the train ticket. He spent the remaining few days alone, rather than with his family or friends. In the afternoon, he would either sleep or read the newspaper. In the evening, he would climb to the top of the Tagore Hill near his home. From there, he would watch the sun go down and the daily-wage labourers return home after a hard day's work. Some of them would be singing songs in Mundari or Kurukh, he couldn't make out which dialect. But he could sense a music in their voices that only emerged when the heart was happy and at home. For a long time, Anirban felt, he had not visited a place like that.

One evening, he went out with a friend and on a sudden urge, bought half a bottle of Old Monk rum. The two drank quietly in the dark of the sprawling Morabadi maidan. By the time they finished, it was way past 10 p.m. Anirban was worried about getting caught. He bought two sachets of Pan Parag, hoping that the masala would mask the stench.

It was 11 p.m. when his mother opened the door. 'What were you doing so late? We were worried,' she said.

'Sorry,' he said and quietly got into his bed.

'What about dinner? I have made egg curry for you. Your father went to the market, especially to get the eggs.'

A whiplash of shame—that's what he felt.

'I have eaten at a friend's place. They forced me, I couldn't refuse,' he lied.

'I will eat the curry tomorrow at lunch,' he said, after a brief pause. This time he wasn't lying.

~

Two days later, before taking the cycle rickshaw to the railway station, he touched his mother's feet. She quietly thrust a 50-rupee note into his palms. 'I know you need the money. And I know that we are not being able to provide as much as you want. But I had saved this for you,' she said.

Anirban wanted to say, 'I think you will need it more.' But he quietly put it in his pocket.

In the evening, the railway waiter came for the dinner order. 'Chicken or vegetarian?' he asked. 'Vegetarian,' Anirban replied.

After dinner, he tried to read Ronald Barthes' *Mythologies* that someone had lent him in the campus. But soon he found himself drifting into slumber. He woke with a start around 2 a.m. Someone seemed to be pulling his suitcase away. Later, he realized it was only a dream.

Back in the hostel, he found Irfan sitting in his room. 'Both Bhatia and you will be gone this summer. Can I borrow your room for some time so that I can concentrate on civil services quietly?' he had asked. Irfan was one of his neighbours and a student of Linguistics from Moradabad. His roommate wasn't going home in the holidays.

Once Bhatia had agreed to the proposal, Anirban had handed him the key.

Irfan was visibly disappointed to see him. 'I wasn't expecting you till next week,' he said. Then he smiled slyly, winked and said, 'I have used your room properly in the last two weeks.' He emphasized the word 'properly' before clearing out.

Anirban couldn't figure out what exactly he meant, though he felt it had something to do with sex. He was happy to have the single room all to himself. He was among the first to be back, three weeks before the holidays ended. For most students, home was an escape not only from the tyranny of course work but also the morning rush for water and the tired food at the mess.

To Anirban, the empty campus felt like an asylum. At home, he felt suffocated by the broken and defeated voices of his parents and the pressure of finding suitable employment and watching them toil with life. He realized how dramatically everything had changed after his father's retirement. When he had had his job with the Bihar police, everything seemed to be all right. But now, inflation had made a sick joke of the pension he received every month.

Life was simpler in the campus during the recess—no queues for the bathroom or the mess. He was surprised when the cook served him two pieces of chicken, instead of one. '*Khao khao, aesh karo, koi nahi hai aaj kal*' he laughingly told Anirban, exhorting him to eat and be merry in the absence of the usual crowd of hostellers. One could also pick up an extra egg for breakfast. Nobody seemed to mind. Even the pamphlet-writers were on vacation.

Anirban noticed that a majority of those who had

stayed back were either civil services' desperadoes taking their last attempt or campus veterans in the dying stages of their doctorates. The campus veterans were a special species. Men and women, who had hung around for the past six years or more and had failed to create something socially acceptable out of life. To them, JNU was like a prison they didn't want to get out of. Here they had a low cost life, camaraderie, even a bit of respect. Outside, they were misfits because their knowledge wasn't exactly marketable. If you had done your PhD on a topic like *India–Mongolia relations and its changing pattern in the emerging global scenario,* think tanks weren't exactly going to throttle each other to get you on their rolls; unless the Embassy of Mongolia itself was interested in you.

As Shubhalok was telling him the other day at the dhaba, Anirban realized that a few students were good enough to win a Ford Foundation scholarship or something worse that many in Red JNU secretly pined for. But they seemed to have a disdain for success and preferred to romance failure. Either they lacked the drive or the desire to run the distance. Guys like them simply enjoyed being driftwood in still waters.

Anirban was beginning to empathize with this lot but he also dreaded becoming one of them. He was aware that he was only a one-year-old in the campus. What worried him was that he himself seemed to be heading nowhere. And that he occasionally enjoyed the idea of going nowhere.

One evening, he saw an India–Pakistan ODI match on TV. The last few overs kept coming back to him like a film in a loop. He sat quietly in the Nilgiri dhaba with a glass of tea. Except for a couple who were busy manhandling each other in the dark, the dhaba was totally empty.

That's when he spotted Purnima Kumari, the quiet girl he had seen making posters in the FT control room during the elections. The one who, he had been told, had taken a midnight train to freedom.

A little more confident than he was before the election, Anirban walked up to her and said, 'Hello! I am Anirban. Do you remember me? I was a SSS councillor candidate for the FTs.'

She laughed. 'Of course, I do. You may not know this but I voted for you too. In fact, I was there when you performed those skits. Some of them were quite funny.'

Anirban wasn't prepared for this. He had come to talk to a reticent girl. He had already conjured up a scenario where he would be nice to her and help her emerge from a shell: much like a hero in a Hindi film helping the leading lady in distress. But Purnima seemed confident enough, a total contrast to what she had appeared to be during the elections.

'You are so chirpy today. That night you were so aloof and serious,' he said, smiling.

'Oh, that night,' she said and laughed. 'You know, I love art work and sometimes I get too involved, even if I am just painting posters.'

'Really?'

'Yes. I think of posters as transient art. They have their own horoscope, their own lines of fate. Some barely live for a few hours before being torn off. Some get smudged in the rain and become tearful versions of themselves. But some live for days, even weeks, defiant like protesters on a fast unto death.'

'Yes,' Anirban nodded in agreement.

'Let us have tea,' she suggested.

'Sure. In fact, my half-empty glass is lying there.'

'Did Mastana tell you about my bad experience with marriage? All that drama of running away from my sasural? Nobody can resist telling such a story.'

The conversation was turning personal.

'He did—not because he was dying to tell me about you, but because I asked him about you.' Anirban was being honest.

'Acchha. Why?'

'Just like that. I was wondering how you could concentrate on your work amidst all the noise. And he gave me the back story,' Anirban said.

Just like that, such an oft-used word to explain something we don't really want to explain.

'Did you find it interesting?'

'I think "intriguing" is a better word,' he replied.

'Okay, let me make a confession. I was aware of you all along.'

'Really?'

'Believe me, I enjoyed your skits.'

Never had things moved so fast with Anirban, especially

with a woman he barely knew. In five minutes flat, she had yanked him out of depression.

They had finished their tea by then. Anirban felt like asking her, '*Ek cup aur?*' But before he could say that she said, 'I think I should resist the temptation of another cup. I will have problems falling asleep,' she said.

'Good night then,' Anirban said.

'Good night. But listen. There is nobody for company these days. If you are not studying late, why don't you come out for tea at 9.30 at night tomorrow?' she said.

Anirban tried to get a mental picture of his schedule. But his mind had turned blank. 'Right,' he said. Walking back, Anirban conceded to himself that he had been swept away by her. He also decided to study for at least eight hours the next day. And he made a promise to himself that he would masturbate only on alternate nights.

18

Purnima properly

DOING COURSE WORK WAS akin to masochism for Anirban. After six hours of reading and writing, he felt drained. He wondered how some of his Bihari seniors managed to study 16 hours a day, as they had confessed to him. But he felt happy nonetheless. Even six was awesome by his modest standards. He felt as though he had completed a mini marathon on one leg: worn-out but uplifted.

Anirban had finished another long-pending task that morning. He took the 666 to Ber Sarai, an urban village located bang opposite the Down Campus. Ber Sarai was a cut-price sanctuary for JNU's outcasts and underclass students. At select homes, you could also get cheap booze deep into the night. You just knocked on a window with money in your palm. Another palm would slip in a small bottle of Solan or Old Monk. The transaction was wordless.

But Ber Sarai was also known for its shops that typed out dissertations and doctorates, peddled photostat copies of civil services materials and notes.

Anirban was aware that UPSC preparations would

begin in right earnest only after he had claimed his Master's degree, two more semesters away. But he had been advised that there was no harm in gathering study material and skimming through the UPSC syllabus whenever there was time.

Life, they say, is all about demand and supply. And nothing typified this more than the photostat industry at Ber Sarai. Photostat copies of books, articles and premium handwritten notes were the lifeblood of the campus, as perhaps in most other colleges and universities across the country.

The business in JNU was run by a dozen shops but one family-run enterprise was miles ahead of the rest. Apart from most sought-after books in international relations, history, economics, sociology, actually the works, they also sold photostat copies of civil services tutorials. They were pretty well-informed. Like a coaching academy, they would even advise the students on what to read and what to avoid, especially for the UPSC exams. The joke went that if one of them ever took the test, he would pass with flying colours.

Having done his bit for the day, Anirban walked up to the Godavari girls' hostel, waiting for Purnima to come out. He was about to go back after hanging around for 10 minutes when he saw her rushing out.

'I am so sorry,' she said. 'I was washing clothes and got late.'

'Washing clothes is a pain,' Anirban said.

'Why? I find it very therapeutic.' She had another point of view.

'What's therapeutic about washing clothes?' he laughed, rather puzzled.

'I can't explain the science of it. But I find it very de-stressing. You know, it is one of those low concentration jobs that allows you to sing or think, whatever you choose, without affecting its quality.'

'So do you sing or think?' he couldn't resist asking.

'Both,' she replied, rather airily. 'Depends on my mood.'

'And what did you do today?'

'Today,' she said, pausing a little, almost pondering whether she should make the thought public or not, 'I sang.'

'What song?'

'You are so curious. Why do you want to know?'

'What makes you so secretive about a song you sang?'

'I don't remember, actually,' she said sheepishly.

Anirban smiled.

By this time, they had almost reached the basketball court. Delhi had been surprised by rain in the past two days. Like a village pond, the campus had burst into life. The trees looked cleaner, greener and happier. Anirban could see two peacocks peeking into the Godavari hostel like slimy voyeurs. Peacocks were plentiful in the capacious campus but they generally hung out in the forested areas. The rains had brought them out of the closet.

The rains, whenever they happened, would do a lot of other things to the campus. The red velvet bugs would be all over the brown earth, their coats so soft you wanted to skin them for a blanket. Of course, the dragonflies, too, buzzed about. They reminded Anirban of his boyhood when he had chased them, and sometimes caught them, tied them with a thread and tried to fly them. Generally, he had ended up breaking their legs.

At a distance, two radical Left student-activists were locked in an animated conversation. The girl was shouting that Marx was a positivist. The boy was screaming he needed to go for a crap. The girl was insisting that the argument wasn't over yet and a true Marxist cannot leave an argument in the middle. In the end, it was clear that her boyfriend was no Marxist for he was scampering in a rather uncomfortable way to the hostel.

The conversation between Purnima and Anirban had stopped temporarily as both were drawn towards the banter between the two voluble Leftists.

'Do you have a girlfriend?' she suddenly asked Anirban.

'No. Not at the moment.' Anirban seemed to be expecting the question but not in so direct a fashion.

'Do you know I have a daughter?' she asked him.

Anirban felt he was free-falling. He went stone quiet.

'Too stunned to say anything?' She wasn't being sarcastic.

'Yes. I am stunned,' he confessed.

'Not many in JNU know this part of my life story,' she said.

'When I ran away from my husband's home, I was carrying his child. When his family discovered that I had given birth to a daughter, they lost interest. Otherwise, they might have fought with me for the baby's custody. We are not divorced yet but he has gone ahead and married again. But I have closed that chapter. For me, that part is over.'

Purnima was casually peeling off her past, like a bandage that had become useless.

'But I had heard something else about your husband.'

'Well, nobody knows the real truth. There are many versions floating about. Tell me, what did you hear? That he has passed away?'

The unmentionable wasn't unmentionable for her.

Anirban just nodded his head gently in affirmation.

'Well, that's one of the rumours. I left him because he was abusive. That's the real reason.'

'Where's your daughter? What's her name?' Anirban asked.

'Dori. She stays with my mother. She is four years old. I talk to her every week. But it isn't easy. We don't have a phone back home and it is strange going to someone's place after 9.30 to wait for a phone call. You know, even going 100 yards away from home at night can be risky in Bihar.'

'I know. We have the same problem. Don't you miss your daughter?'

'Of course I do. But I tell myself, I am doing all this for her. I am prepared to face the world, Anirban. Mark my words! I will have a good job within three years. Then my daughter can stay with me.'

Then Purnima cupped her cheeks with her hands and said, 'Now tell me about yourself.'

'My life isn't half as exciting as yours. You will get bored,' he said, rather tamely but honestly.

'I won't,' she said, and pressed her hand against his. Anirban was surprised. He couldn't make out if the gesture was an expression of intent. As it had happened in Geetha's case, he wasn't used to women talking so freely about themselves. And he was certainly not accustomed to getting his hands squeezed in the dark.

'Okay. Tell me the most exciting thing you have done in your life?'

'Well, along with a few friends, I once stopped a train from leaving a railway station.'

'Arrey! How? What did you do?'

'Well, we just whipped out a few lathis to scare the guard and stopped him from waving the green flag. But it is quite a complicated story actually.'

'That sounds interesting. But it wasn't exactly your initiative. You were part of a mob?'

'Well, it wasn't a mob; just four-five friends.'

'It may not have appeared like a mob to you because you were a part of it. For everybody else in the station, it was a mob or a gang,' she said.

Anirban nodded his head in agreement, rather reluctantly. *Perhaps she is right*, he thought.

'Actually, I am interested in knowing something. What's the most exciting thing you did on your own?'

'Well, I kissed my girlfriend even as all three of us were walking together.'

'Who was the third person?'

'Her mother,' Anirban smiled.

'How did you do it?' She sounded genuinely curious.

'Madness, I would say. You know the sort of stupid thing you do when you are in love. You act without thinking of consequences. She was walking behind her mother and I was walking behind her. I just sneaked up to her, kissed her on her cheek and moved on. It was as if nothing had happened.'

'Very brave,' she laughed.

'Well, you know if you are in love, you just walk on air. You just live for the moment.'

'I wouldn't know that. I have never been in love that way,' she said.

'I have. Or, at least I have imagined myself to be. And then it doesn't even matter if you have money or not. Thankfully, by some strange coincidence, all my girlfriends have been rich so far,' he took shelter in levity.

'You are sure it was a coincidence?' she was teasing him now.

Anirban ducked that one. Changing the topic, he said, 'I am the only son of a retired honest cop. The key word here is honest. Once we were middle-class. After Baba's retirement, we are lower middle-class. And we will stay that way until I get a job. In that sense, my situation is pretty similar to yours.'

'Do you have any sisters?'

'Yes. One.'

'Is she married?'

'Yes.'

'Then why do you feel weighed down by pressure? You don't have any major responsibilities. Your parents are okay. All you have got to do is take care of yourself. I am sure you can do that.'

'I must. But I am getting waylaid. I often lose focus and end up doing things I shouldn't be doing.'

'That happens to all of us occasionally. You are old enough to make your own decisions and then stand by them. That's how you become a grown-up.'

Was that a slight? Is she telling me that I am not a grown-up? Anirban wondered. But before he could come to a conclusion, he had a question to reply to.

'Do you have a girlfriend?'

'No.'

'Sure?'

'Why do you ask?'

'Just like that. I don't have a boyfriend. And I don't think I will have one for a long, long time,' she said.

And then she looked rather meaningfully at Anirban. And before he could realize what she meant by that look, he found her lips were pressing against his.

When she had stopped kissing him, she asked Anirban, 'Are you surprised?'

'Of course, especially since you just said you didn't want a boyfriend for a long, long time.'

'I mean what I say. What does a kiss have to do with a boyfriend?'

'Nothing? Is that what you are saying?'

'To me, a boyfriend means some kind of emotional commitment. A kiss doesn't need commitment; it only needs desire and the courage to express that desire.'

So what does she want? Anirban wasn't sure. Was she a friend who wanted to fuck? Anirban didn't know. He was not the sort of guy equipped to make a move on that front. Speed-mating was not his style.

'You know what, I knew very little about sex till I got married. When I was 10 years old, one of my chachajis, who is dead now, used to run his fingers over my body. I didn't know what to do. Now I realize I was being molested. Do you know I was a virgin when I got married?'

Some questions are like confessions. Anirban understood this was one of them. He kept quiet.

Purnima continued, 'I stayed with my husband for just six months. He wasn't caring but had a huge libido. We made love almost every night. I hated it at first, then started enjoying the damn thing. And now I am on this forced celibacy. In fact, that's the only thing I miss about marriage.

'I hate words like love. How do you know that a person loves you for sure? There are no signs or indicators. Lust is so much easier to understand or accept. The body offers evidence. You cannot lie about it.' Her voice had turned into a low whisper. Anirban felt she was poised to mate there and then.

But she surprised him again.

'I must go now,' she said. 'And thanks for the company.'

After she left, Anirban wondered briefly whether, like him, she was also going to masturbate.

19

An affair unspools

The vacation was over. Classes had resumed. Anirban was coming back from the centre after attending a lecture by Sabyasachi Bhattacharya on the Swadeshi movement when he saw some kind of hullaballoo outside the hostel gate. A middle-aged woman in a blue salwar-kurta was showering the choicest of abuses with amazing abandon. A bunch of students, who had gathered around her, were sniggering. The chowkidar was trying to shoo her away.

'*Irfan ko bulao, andar hoga*' she was shouting, demanding that Irfan be called out immediately.

'*Madam, aap udhar, side mein bathiye. Ladka gaya hai, aata hi hoga,*' said the chowkidar, probably lying about the fact that someone had been sent inside to call Irfan.

'*Pandrah minutes se tum yahi keh rahe ho. Kahan hai woh?*' she demanded, berating the chowkidar for trying to fob her off.

But Irfan, who was cowering like a mouse in his room, was in no mood to come out. She left after an hour but not before creating a huge tamasha. By the time she had finally gone away, everybody in the hostel knew that Irfan was involved with a shady lower-class woman.

Then the story tumbled out. Irfan was travelling in a DTC bus one night. The woman was sitting by his side. Irfan first touched her hand, taking care to make it appear unintended. When she didn't move away, he felt emboldened. Slowly, he started groping her northwards. By the time they had reached Prithviraj Road, he realized she had shifted slightly closer to him. And by the time they reached Laxmi Nagar, his fingers were gently stroking her fully aroused nipples.

Before getting down at bus stop near the huge Bhikaji Cama Place complex, she softly asked him if he wanted to come with her. Irfan, already hard and horny, agreed with alacrity. She took him to her shack, plied him with hot tea and the next hour or so, fucked him relentlessly. She was very aggressive, often taunting Irfan, and demanding if that was all he had. Irfan, by his own admission, pumped her like a porn star.

In the moments of post-coital tenderness that followed, Irfan found out that she was a fourth-grade MCD employee, a street janitor. That she had separated from her whisky-addict husband who was not only unfaithful but also unemployed of late.

Irfan claimed to have slept with several men and women before. But he had tasted something different and heady in this risky business. He didn't know whether it was the rush of an adventure or the risk of sleeping with an unknown woman in the times of HIV that he found so irresistible.

He could have turned the encounter into a 'it happened one night' kind of thing and left it at that: with a kiss on her bruised cheek and a pat on her bum. But he didn't. Irfan became a lover, visiting her every week, even bringing her occasional gifts like hawai chappals and cheap bras bought at Rs 50 per 100 grams at the weekly market in Munirka. She conveyed her love and gratitude by serving him spicy mutton curry swamped in mustard oil.

She was the reason why he had asked for the keys to Anirban's room in the holidays.

But one day, the ruffians of her underclass colony confronted Irfan. '*Kya hero, har Sunday maza marne aa jaate ho,*' they growled, pointing out that Irfan seemed to be having a lot of fun every Sunday in their territory. They even slapped him around a couple of times. And when another guy, rather menacingly, threatened to chop off a beloved part of his anatomy, he immediately realized all good things must come to an end.

Like hundreds of others in the campus, Irfan was also taking the civil services entrance exams. Like everybody else, he fancied his chances and didn't want to get involved in a police case. He stopped visiting her. And that's why she came calling that afternoon. The woman never filed a police complaint but her visit ensured that the incident passed into campus folklore.

A smart-alec coined a pet name for Irfan and it stuck with him for the rest of his stay in the campus: Jamadar babu.

20

The first time

IT HAD BEEN six weeks since Purnima had kissed Anirban below the flourishing tree just outside Godavari hostel.

They had bonded since then.

First, it was just post-dinner chats over tea. Then it stretched to post-breakfast conversations and sometimes pre-lunch natters over nimboo-pani. Post-lunch chats would seamlessly blend into pre-dinner talks, followed by post-dinner exchanges.

Rajesh Khanna films. Mohan Rakesh short stories. Nagarjun's poetry. Mithila paintings. The state of women in rural Bihar. Her childhood friends. His classmates. Classroom lectures. Her daughter. His ex-girlfriends and their mothers. Ganesh Pyne. Naxalites. Svetlana and Bhatia. Why he loved cricket and sleeveless blouses. Why jeans are better than salwar-kurtas. Gandhi. Civil services syllabus. A possible career in art.

They had the world to discuss.

Everything that matters. And everything that doesn't.

They belonged to different backgrounds and were

shaped by different pasts. But instinctively, they trusted each other. That was the key to their connection.

Anirban now began to avoid FT meetings. He wanted to focus on just two things: course work and Purnima, with a dash of civil services background preparations. There was no space left for anything else.

There is a time when the girl you like is beginning to like you. This was that time, he felt.

Of course, sometimes he would still think about Geetha. Anirban was aware that she was committed to someone else now. He hardly came across her. Or, maybe, his routine had changed. In bed, he would often make a comparative analysis of life with Purnima and Geetha, sometimes with both. He would match their attributes and his compatibility with them. It was a fantasy he feasted on.

For the campus, Anirban and Purnima had become an item. That was an assumption. After Purnima's blunt confessional, 'I don't want to fall in love with anybody' on the first evening they had spent together outside the Godavari hostel, Anirban had decided he would not make the first move on taking the relationship to the next level. Barring the sole kiss, which Purnima had initiated nights ago, there was nothing physical about their togetherness.

He loved her smell, the way she had handled the odds, faced the world. Sometimes he would steal a glance at her small, coy breasts. But he also wondered if she wanted him the same way. After all, they had quite a few opportunities. She had come to his room on several occasions. They had been alone so many times. But nothing like that had happened.

Then, one afternoon when he was about to leave for class after lunch, he heard a soft knock on the back door. Bhatia had left the room a few minutes back, so it couldn't be him, Anirban knew.

He was thinking about keeping quiet in case it was one of those love-birds looking for passage. Then he heard a low, familiar voice asking him to open the door, '*Darwaza kholo, kya kar rahe ho?*'

It was Purnima in a white skirt, not one of her favourite outfits. And a red top.

'Hi,' she said.

That was last word she spoke for some time.

The moment he shut the door, she grabbed his backside with an intrusive left hand. Then she swivelled him around and caressed his cheeks before focusing her attention on his eager lips. Anirban returned the favour this time. Soon they were treating each other's lips like tangy nimboo achaar.

Anirban threw off her T-shirt in a hurry as if it was infected with some virus. He plucked the bra off her shoulders and immediately noticed that her breasts defied gravity.

Purnima loved playing games in bed. Like a kid walking on tiptoes, she let her left hand journey southwards. She seemed delighted in discovering that an upright object prevented her journey further downwards. Softly, she purred a 'meeow', and then tried to grab that stiff part of her partner's anatomy. Anirban was wearing a suffocating pair of Avis jeans, not some soft cotton pyjamas. Purnima appeared to find the situation both amusing and vexing.

She started fiddling with the obdurate zip, leading Anirban to believe that he was going to get a job of some kind.

To his mild dismay, he found she wasn't intending on doing anything like that. Purnima had something else up her sleeve.

'Do you have a name for him?' she pointed downwards with her eyes.

He blushed, then recovered to say, 'No, but we can think of something right now.'

'Suggest something,' she said. Her voice was hoarse. In fact, thought Anirban somewhat distractedly, she sounded a bit like a donkey with a bad cough.

'How about Bhaiyaji or Raja babu,' he said.

'I like the first one. I can ask in front of anybody, *Aur Bhaiyaji kaise hain?*' she whispered.

'I want to give you some names too,' he said.

'What?' She seemed very keen to hear one.

'I would call the twins Seeta aur Geeta. The one on the right is Seeta, and the other is Geeta. How do you like that?'

She moaned softly in affirmation because by then, Anirban had started fondling Geeta. 'And I have a name for the better half of Bhaiyaji…'

'What?' she seemed to be genuinely curious.

'Rani sahiba.'

'Nice,' she said.

Anirban was giddy with excitement. Driven by pure instinct, he decided to bow before the queen. But Purnima cut him short with a terse *'Rani sahiba abhi so rahin hain,'* telling him in no uncertain words that the queen was sleeping.

Clearly, she believed in foreplay. Lots and lots of foreplay. Sex for Purnima, Anirban realized, was a game full of uninhibited, dirty talk—perhaps a carry-over from her marital experience. She seemed to be enjoying the fact that her man was much more desperate than her and that she was in control. Anirban was unpractised in the art of delayed gratification but theoretically trained.

Friends in Ranchi had told him that *bistar me ladkiyan do tarah ki hoti hain—thandi aur randi*. Meaning that in bed there are two kinds of girls: cold, and bold like a whore. They had also explained during one of those hugely illuminating addas that contrary to popular wisdom, size didn't matter. What mattered was durability.

So he slowly kissed her, both in public and pubic places, tasting even those parts that obviously needed a good razor. And eventually, he had her joyfully parted below.

She started returning his thrusts soon enough. One of her rapturous but flailing hands struck a bottle of Dettol lying on the study table. The loosely capped bottle fell on the bed, its contents spilling over on to her reposing bra. A sharp smell of antiseptic enveloped the room as they continued to rock back and forth.

Suddenly, someone knocked at the door. They stopped, dripping beads of sweat in consternation. The knocking continued as if the visitor was sure that Anirban was inside. But eventually, he went away.

Fucking in a hostel room is much like farting: one must avoid surround sound and do it as quietly as possible. But chances are people will get to know anyway. They kept fucking soundlessly like a movie on mute. And after he had come, gushing and gasping, Anirban realized that his partner had made no similar noises of gratification.

But Purnima didn't complain. Soon, her middle finger got busy performing a task generally done in solitude.

Anirban watched her contented breasts greedily as she put on her clothes. When she was about to open the door and leave, he pulled her back into his arms. He kissed her on the back of her head and drew in the faint fragrance of Cantharidine hair oil, a smell that was a part of his childhood memory of his sister and mother. Now that he had found that smell in a woman he had just slept with, he felt more connected with her. It was as if the smell of that hair oil had a special intimacy, a kind of secret code that made her someone he knew better, and that revealed more of her to him.

She understood that he was soaking in the scent of her hair. And smiled to herself. When he let her go, she opened the door and did not look back. Perhaps she knew that he wanted to see her face one last time. And that's what she did not want.

That night, Anirban was swarmed by images as he closed his eyes. He enjoyed replaying every moment of the afternoon again and again. But alongside the erotic images also came a bunch of feelings. He couldn't place his finger on what exactly they meant. Was he falling in love? Or, maybe something similar that he didn't have a word for? He felt muddled inside.

That night he had seen something new written on the

door opposite his room. '*What lies before us and what lies behind us are tiny matters compared to what lies between us.*' He felt comforted by those words in a curious sort of way. They became his lullaby for the night.

21

EMS

ANIRBAN SPOTTED GEETHA Kasturi on his way towards the SSS building. She seemed to be lost in her thoughts but perked up at the sight of Anirban.

'Hi! Long time,' she said, rather cheerfully.

''My thoughts exactly,' Anirban replied.

'EMS is delivering a lecture at the SSS around 4 o'clock. That would be just after your Bipan Chandra class. Would love to see you there,' she said, emphasizing the word 'love'.

Geetha could be utterly charming when she wanted to.

'Sure,' Anirban said aloud. *Never* is what he meant.

But when Bipan's lecture was over, Anirban saw Ms Kasturi outside the classroom, asking every student to come for the talk by the great Communist leader of Kerala. Anirban felt trapped. Rather than act rude, he decided to attend the meet.

Despite his pronounced stammer and advanced age, EMS Namboodripad was speaking with fervour and everybody, especially the young cadres, were listening with rapt attention. That's when an old student, Josy (everybody knew his name by the evening) got up and started shouting. He wanted EMS to explain some of the CPM's controversial policies in Kerala.

Before he could complete his long question, two senior SFI student leaders jumped on him. One of them twisted his hand to the back, locked him in an unshakeable grip and dragged him out of the hall. Another protester was escorted out in a similar manner. Obviously, the stakes were too high for the SFI leaders. Despite the mild setback at the polls, JNU was still seen as a secure Left bastion. The campus party bosses had to do whatever was necessary to maintain that image.

Anirban was stunned by this muzzling of dissent. 'So when it comes to putting on a show for their beloved leader, democracy is taken out for a walk,' he heard someone wisecrack in the back. He quietly walked out of the hall.

Ms Kasturi was standing in the doorway. 'Where are you going?' she smiled as she asked.

'I am going to sleep. Probably that would be more enlightening,' he replied and walked away.

22

A strange love story

BACK IN THE hostel, he was about to reach for his key when he saw the door was ajar. Inside, Svetlana and Bhatia were listening to songs on the Walkman, one headphone apiece.

On seeing Anirban, Bhatia said, 'Hey, weren't you supposed to have come earlier?'

'Yes, but was held up at a meeting. What's happening here?'

'I am teaching her Hindi through film songs. We listen to the same song. She writes down the words she cannot understand. Then I explain it to her.'

'Nice,' Anirban said.

They left within five minutes of his arrival. Sensing this as a good opportunity, Anirban sat down to study though he found himself drawn towards an Alistair MacLean thriller, *Fear is the Key*, lying on Bhatia's bed.

After 20 minutes or so, he heard a soft knock. *So, Bhatia is back*, he thought. Instead, it was his neighbour Nikhil-ji.

Nikhil-ji was the son of an upper caste, Bhumihar to be precise, landlord with over 700 acres of land in fertile

Bhojpur. His father was on the most-wanted list of the Naxalites who were locked in a bitter no-holds-barred battle with the zamindars of the region.

Unlike many other sons of landlords who were packed off to study in the convent schools of Patna and Calcutta, Nikhil-ji had grown up in Arrah, the heart of Bhojpur district. He was a bright student. One of his class teachers had told him that he could easily make a career in physics. But his father wanted him to take care of the land. That part was written in stone.

One of his uncles had gifted him Maxim Gorky's *Mother* and Leo Tolstoy's *War and Peace*, in Hindi of course, on his seventeenth birthday. Reading them, he developed a fondness for Russia, even though it had morphed into the Soviet Union since then. It helped that India and USSR were in the middle of a torrid love affair. Nikhil-ji pleaded with his father to let him study the Russian language. The five years at JNU was the equivalent of his 'baby's day out'.

Nikhil-ji had a gentleness and dignity that immediately forced everyone to add the respectful suffix, ji, when they spoke of him. From all accounts, he was a good student of the Russian language. Negotiating the new campus culture was far more difficult for a 'kasba' boy like him.

The kasba and small town was a state of mind that boys and girls brought to the city like an inseparable pet. But the city wouldn't allow them to keep it. The city mocked and taunted the small town inside the small-towners. Some small-town boys wanted to become the city: taste it, blend with it. But that wasn't easy. The city was typified by individualism, a sense of superiority and poise. The small town was rough-cut. The tentative and the indecisive ones resorted to collective clinginess. The more individualistic looked for power and assurance in a group. Some sought refuge in a fake public school accent, or in pretending to enjoy classical music concerts organized by SpicMacay. But the more they tried to blend, the more miserably they failed. They were mocked at and pushed away.

Defeated and dejected, many would retreat into a shell. They were afraid to speak up in public, even in small groups, afraid that their pronunciation, where 'is' became 'eej' and 'was' became 'waaj', would draw sardonic smiles. Among all the things they feared most was humiliation. Every day was a battle to protect and preserve self-esteem. The battle was real but the reasons often imagined. It is what is vulgarly, and rather simplistically, called a complex.

Actually, the city and the small town were not separate, watertight compartments. And that was part of the problem. Many were neither small town nor city. They wanted to belong to both of them and at the same time.

The girls on the campus were different from what they had come across at home. They were certainly not the Meena Kumaris, or even the Hema Malinis, they had come to idealize and idolize. In small towns, girls were always required to use the dupatta, the stole that covered their honour.

Here many girls had dumped that basic accessory. Discarding the dupatta was a triumph against patriarchy, a mini milestone of life. Rather than lower their eyes when a guy stared at their breasts, they would stare back, forcing him to look elsewhere.

Some boys would wonder aloud in the mess how a girl could allow a bra strap to hang out so irresponsibly. Back home, they had been told *Je hasal se phasal*—if a girl laughs, then she is interested. Here the girls were laughing all the time. The boys claimed to hate these girls but they would have done anything to chat with any of them.

Nikhil-ji, however, was comfortable in his own skin, firmly rooted in his rural moorings. He had come to learn Russian, not to transform himself into an urban Indian. He was proud of what he was and he wanted to stay that way. He wasn't out to win popularity contests; lovers were barred from passing through his room much to their dismay.

Nikhil-ji was also an introvert. He didn't make friends easily although he would occasionally visit DU where a couple of his schoolmates were allegedly studying. Sometimes when Bhatia wasn't around, he would knock at Anirban's door.

'Can I disturb you for two minutes?' he would say while he blended his mixture of tobacco and lime, the preferred way of consuming 'khaini' in many parts of north India.

'Of course,' Anirban would reply. He liked Nikhil-ji, except for the fact that he did not hesitate to spit anywhere and everywhere. He enjoyed Nikhil-ji's village stories and the fact, unlike many others, that he did not try to recast himself as a smart young urban Indian, which to him primarily meant wearing baggy trousers, eating pizza at Nirula's, watching English movies at Chanakya and saying, 'fuck' or 'shit' in every third sentence.

But that day, Nikhil-ji had come to narrate a love story. His own.

'Life has a way of making you look stupid,' he said.

Anirban was shocked. 'What happened,' he asked with genuine curiosity.

'My story is very complicated. And I don't know how to deal with it.'

'Unless you tell me what happened, how can I even try?'

'You know Pragya, right? You must have seen her with me at the dhaba?' Nikhil-ji said.

Anirban hadn't. But he said, yes, just to let the conversation keep flowing.

'You know, she is my classmate. In the past few months we had become sort of close friends. She is married, so I thought, *Chalo girlfriend ka koi confusion nahi hai.* But now, Pragya says that she has fallen in love with me, wants to divorce her husband and get married.'

'You got to watch out, Nikhil-ji. This could be a trap,' Anirban smiled.

'Listen to the full story first. And please don't share this information with anyone,' he said.

Anirban felt like saying, *don't trust me so much*, but he didn't want to spoil the moment.

'You see, Pragya was forced into marriage. In fact, she is not the only victim in this whole story. Her husband is a victim too,' Nikhil-ji was being very mysterious.

'This is very interesting. Is it something like the *pakadua byah*, those shotgun weddings?' Curiosity was now beginning to kill Anirban. In Bihar, rich, eligible bachelors are often kidnapped and forcibly married off under duress. Shotgun weddings is common practice, a well-established cottage industry.

'No. This is different, only worse. This guy was working on his PhD under Pragya's brother in Delhi University. He wasn't a good student. After three years, her brother started berating him, saying he wasn't good enough to get a doctorate. Gradually, Pragya's brother managed to convince the guy that he must leave the project and try his hand at something else. Or, else he must find another guide.

'Much to Pragya's dismay, her brother cut a deal with his student: marry my sister for no dowry and I will not only help you finish your thesis but also try to get you a job. The poor chap agreed. Pragya told me that she couldn't oppose the marriage because she felt obliged to do whatever her elder brother asked her. After all, he had taken care of her ever since their parents died.

'Now four years after marriage, and having spent these months among more modern and liberated girls, she realizes how she became a victim. Now she wants to break free and become a survivor. She wants to divorce the guy and start a new chapter in life.'

'Quite an incredible story,' Anirban agreed. Back home he was aware of many strange marriages and stranger love stories, but this seemed to take the cake. 'Nikhil-ji, all I am going to tell you is, please tread softly...*phoonk phoonk ke kadam rakhiye.* I hope you don't get dragged into a dirty marital squabble.'

'Look, if I don't get involved, how can I say that I really

love Pragya. Don't you think that I must help her in this time of need?'

'Do what you think is right. But consider every move carefully.' Anirban was trying to warn him without being too pushy.

Nikhil-ji was on the point of saying something when Bhatia walked in. Nikhil-ji mumbled a weak hello, and quietly moved out of the room.

'What was he saying? I seemed to have interrupted a conversation,' Bhatia said.

'Nothing special, just small talk,' Anirban lied.

He stepped out of the room and went to the dhaba. He saw Robi, Jack and Yogendra there. They were cheery and chirpy. 'Please meet two future civil servants of India,' Robi said. Anirban was taken aback. He was not aware that the latest IAS results were out and both Jack and Yogendra were among the successful. Almost reflexively, he offered his hand in congratulations.

'We are going out to get smashed. Why don't you come with us?' Jack said.

'I would love to,' he replied, 'but I am neck-deep in term papers.'

23

Hostel raids

LIKE WHOREHOUSES, JNU hostels were prone to late-night raids. Wardens, along with the administrative support staff, would morph into campus cops and would go about knocking at every door, checking on illegal guests and girlfriends.

Girlfriends were rarely found; most girls who came over would tiptoe out by midnight or so. The raids took place around 3 a.m. Once, a girl caught during such a raid claimed she had no memory of how she got in there. It was her way of mocking the administration. And when she stuck to her stand, the authorities could do nothing, except fine her Rs 50.

On another occasion, a girl escaped from the second floor, climbing down a sewer pole. She was a member of the mountaineering club and an expert at rock climbing.

The main objective of hostel raids was catching 'illegal guests'. JNU hostels weren't just hostels; they were low-cost dharamshalas too. Apart from the hostellers who lived there, they were also refuge to hundreds of 'illegal' students flirting with luck in the big city. These 'illegal' guests were usually friends of an inmate and were either preparing for the civil services or for the forthcoming JNU entrance exams. They slept on the floor of their benefactor's room.

Some guests would spend up to a couple of years in a room, leaving many confused as to who was the guest and who the actual occupant.

But sometimes, a late-night hostel raid was prompted by a curious reason: a shortage of plates in the mess room. The lunch and dinner plates, which resembled railway thalis, often went missing by the dozens. This often created a long queue during lunch and dinner time. Residents could not be served till one batch had finished their meal and the plates were washed. The result was a regular ruckus over the plates. How long could you stand in a queue for bad food and how many times could you read a pamphlet?

The hostellers themselves were the main reason behind the missing plates. Many of them took the plates filled with food back to their rooms and, rather thoughtlessly, left the empty plates in the balcony of their rooms rather than bring them back to the mess. Over a period, this created a shortfall in the mess.

On one such occasion, 34 plates were found in a hosteller's balcony. Some of them had not been returned for months, and colonies of plants had grown on many of them. In some cases, the plates had turned green with moss. The guy responsible for the act was a radical Left intellectual, known to read his books everywhere except in the library. He read them at the dhaba, at the bus stop and while walking to the campus. He once fell from a DTC bus because he was reading and trying to hop in at the same time. He was taken to the dispensary. It is said that he continued reading his book even when they were putting on the bandage. He was fined Rs 500 for all the misery he had caused to the rest of the hostel. Ten of the thirt-four thalis were thrown away. They were beyond cleaning.

But one hostel raid that had the warden knocking on Anirban's door had a far more unpalatable reason: homophobia. A week before the raid, an outsider had come to the Periyar hostel. Dressed in a flashy red shirt and blue trousers, he was brash enough to enter the common room and ask around, if there were any men interested in other men.

Homosexuality was one of those don't-know-don't-ask sort of topics. In a campus of 2,000-odd students, it was unlikely that a few were not gays. But nobody was identified as gay. Heterosexual lovers, who found release in the bushes, claimed having witnessed men making out with men in similar dark surroundings but nobody seemed to be able to identify who they were.

There was one lesbian couple though. Both were north Indians but from different religions. But that was not the reason why they finally were torn apart. One of them was married off much against her wish. Her lover, one learnt many years later, committed suicide.

There were no similar identifiable male couples.

The outsider, who had boldly gone around enquiring about members of his tribe, allegedly entered a Nepali student's room. After a brief chit-chat, he rose from his seat and kissed him.

The good-looking Nepali was shocked out of his wits and threw him off. But he did not create a scene. The outsider left the hostel. Late at night, he returned to the hostel and pleaded with several students to let him sleep there for the night.

One generous student agreed. But after the lights were switched off, he found the stranger fondling his pyjamas. Taken aback, he screamed.

His neighbours rushed in to find out what had happened. Nobody knew what to do with the outsider. One of the chowkidars, a burly gentleman from Rohtak who generally dealt sternly with intruders, was surprisingly accommodating. 'I will escort him out of the campus,' he told the warden.

He returned the next morning.

24

Tiananmen and Mandal

THE 1989 TIANANMEN Square massacre was a godsend to the anti-SFI lobby. For once the men in red knickers, endlessly bellicose on American excesses in Vietnam, were pushed on to the backfoot. Some, out of sheer habit, issued denials of certitude but others preferred to remain tongue-tied. Despite the shocking display of authoritarianism, the SFI remained conveniently vague about the incident where hundreds of protesters, many of them college students, were killed in cold blood. After a point, all ideologies devolve into some kind of faith and breed their own dogmas and gods. This was an example.

Information trickled out of China as fast as water from taps in desert towns. But the rationing only fuelled the hunger of those who felt that the Communist state had stepped way out of line. There were plenty of animated late-night discussions in the hostels on the killings, which ostensibly were done to protect the revolution. In the campus, every anti-SFI group now had a handle and a hammer to beat down the Big Brother of the campus. And they had a common cause to unite.

Soon an amorphous anti-SFI front named Solidarity, of which the Free Thinkers' party was also a part, burst into life. Anirban had long stepped away from politics but his vote was among those that powered the newbie formation to a shock triumph over the SFI. If only the Chinese politburo had known of the repercussions of their actions in the most unshakeable bastions on earth!

A year later, the Mandal Commission Report's implementation by the VP Singh government at the Centre shocked JNU even more, shaking its very core. The report's implementation allowed 27 per cent reservations for OBCs (other backward classes) in government jobs, fuelling the deep anxieties among upper-caste students in times when a sarkari job wasn't just a stairway to heaven. It was heaven itself in capital letters.

Many campus intellectuals dismissed the anti-Mandal agitation as a reactionary upper-caste movement. The Student's Union resigned over the issue.

For years, JNU prided itself on being immune to change. Many liked to believe that the campus was an island. In about two decades of its life, JNU had created a distinct identity of its own, which was noticeably different from every other university in the country. It was incredibly politically aware with more shades of the Red than the Nerolac paints catalogue could show. It was free of violence, ragging and eve-teasing, well almost.

Molestation cases were rare but not totally unheard of. In the winter of 1986, a girl was groped by 'an outsider' on her way back alone from the library at night. Some years later, a small group of students set a Maruti car on fire. Nobody was caught. The car owners were 'outsiders' trying to molest a girl. Many students applauded the students for this alleged act of militancy. Most probably it was a brawl that had turned ugly.

But the most well-known case of molestation took place in a hostel room where a PhD student tried to molest a foreign student. This incident turned political because it had taken place in the room of a student who was a senior member in a newly formed party.

Strangely, in the middle of a charged GBM, the girl jumped on the stage. Identifying herself as the survivor, she said, 'I don't want anyone to make an issue out of it.' The accused, however, was rusticated from the university and the incident died a quick death.

Caste or religion weren't preferred tools to negotiate life in JNU. Over the years, the campus had created its own social and political ethos which filtered down to new batches of students who came with their own baggage of prejudices and predilections. Within a semester or two, they would internalize the JNU way of life. Of course, there were exceptions. But they were never numerous enough to challenge or change the existing way.

The anti-Mandal agitation proved that JNU's internationalism and modernity was no match to India's primeval formation: caste.

The agitation started a few months after the new batch of students had arrived that year. Suddenly faced with a career-threatening situation, without having been tutored to the JNU way, many of them formed the core of the protests. But the truth is that even some older upper-caste students, feeling threatened by the change, welcomed old beasts and allowed themselves to be carried away by the storm.

For this bunch, the students' union and the campus political parties became irrelevant. For them, the world was divided into those who were in support of the movement and those who were not.

Everybody saw the situation from the prism of their own social background. Some upper-caste students were always driven by a sense of scorn against SC and ST students. The general view was that these students have it very easy. 'They get so many chances to clear the exams,' was a common gripe. Whenever a student, not known to be particularly bright, cleared the civil services, eyebrows would be raised and smirks released. 'Check out his caste, he must be an SC,' someone would remark. Discreeet enquiries would be made. And often the rumour mills went on overdrive.

Post-MCR, everyone started identifying students from an OBC or a non-OBC point of view. There was a coalescing of the upper castes as a community in the dhabas and the mess. Many of those who hardly ever spoke to each other became part of a group united by a common interest.

The OBC students, too, gathered under the common umbrella of self-interest. They would sit together in one corner and eat food as if trying to find strength in numbers. But it was evident that compared to the general population, their percentage was ridiculously low.

For the upper-caste civil services aspirant, life centred around one irreplaceable dream: the IAS. It didn't matter whether his rank was 1 or 1,000. For him, the world was divided into two fixed compartments: those who saw their names on the UPSC notice board after the final results were declared and those who didn't. The difference between the two was the difference between heaven and hell, between Rs 20 lakhs as dowry or one-tenth of that, between a tip-top, convent-educated trophy wife, or just a leftover that came his family's way. The stakes were extremely high; the rank also linked to a sister's marriage, to a father's social prestige. This is what a student from Bihar or Uttar Pradesh—and he was an upper-caste guy eight out of ten times—saw in the civil services exams.

That's why the UPSC was an obsession for them. That's why they focused on it more intensely than an Olympian for a medal. That's why they slogged for 16 hours a day. The prospect of being a District Collector worked like an invisible drug they were all high on.

Some succumbed to the pressure and cracked. They would complain of dizziness, chest pain, sleeplessness, and every other stress-related disease. Those who found their names missing from the list after having appeared for the interview were the worst hit. They would slide into gloom. Then they would haul themselves out of the slump and gather themselves again. Sometimes, and this was not rare, a student would be unlucky enough to be rejected thrice after the interview.

Getting over the UPSC experience was like negotiating

heartbreak. Only a thousand times worse. There was a harrowing sense of losing something almost in your grasp, so close you could almost picture yourself barking orders at subordinates as a district collector and distributing largesse to flood victims like an emperor. All that was lost forever. They were left with a terrifying sense of emptiness, of being denied something fundamental to their existence and a long battle with a demon called depression.

With the coming of Mandal, these students saw this world slipping away. The MCR's implementation triggered off a major subterranean fear within. Nobody wanted to face the fact that out of every student who cleared the exam, 20 did not. Of the 1,50,000 who took the exams, only 900-odd got in anyway. What they saw was that the number of reserved seats would go up further, once the OBC reservation kicked in. Like a virus, this fear took control of their lives.

Many of these candidates saw the development as a conspiracy planned by some fiendish brain to deny them what they felt was their birthright. They also felt betrayed because an upper-caste prime minister had put the seal on it.

Yet there was still no real direction or catalyst to the anger that was building up against the MCR. It was the self-immolation attempt of Rajeev Goswami, a Delhi University student, which turned the agitation into a bush-fire that engulfed several parts of India in the winter of 1990.

DTC buses were hijacked by the protesters, their

windscreens smashed. You could see tyres burning all over the city. Hostels in Delhi University became war rooms. Several JNU students interested in the agitation moved to those parts.

The MCR was a litmus test for the Free Thinkers. So far, the party had relished being the first alternative to the official Left in the campus. It was primarily a party of the young urban and semi-urban, convent-educated students whose self-image was secular and liberal. The implementation of MCR meant there was a new elephant in the room that the party had to parley with. Old-timers like Jack and Yogendra had joined the civil services a few months back. They were not around to guide the party anymore.

It was time for a new leadership to take charge. But the FT was in a dilemma, fragmented in its view. The mood in the campus, especially among the upper-caste/middle-class students, was aggressively militant and aggressive. The anti-Mandal agitation had taken off the veneer of deceit that JNU displayed on caste. What was subterranean became explicit. MCR underlined that ideology was skin-deep but caste ran deeper.

Anirban found out that most Free Thinkers had turned into strong anti-Mandal supporters. No one knew what the movement was going to achieve. Everybody wanted more chances to appear for the civil services and an extension of age for those appearing in all competitive exams. For most students, this is what it had boiled down to.

When Mastana saw him sitting with Purnima one day,

he took Anirban aside and told him, 'You can do all this later. But this moment in history will go away. We must fight together to stop MCR from being implemented. Tomorrow, there's a major rally at Boat Club. The farmer's leader Mahendra Singh Tikait and his supporters will be there. You must come.'

It was more an order, less a request. 'I will,' Anirban said without any genuine enthusiasm. Lovers have a way of detaching themselves from the surroundings. And Anirban was in that state of mind.

But he also knew that saying 'no' at this point would be inappropriate. Sometimes it is imperative to run with the pack; or be prepared to be seen as a traitor.

He went to the Boat Club riding pillion on Mastana's motorcycle. Neither of them wore a helmet. There wasn't a single traffic cop in sight. They parked the mobike in a Congress MP's home—Mastana knew him as he was a fellow Rajput from Bihar.

The Boat Club was a sea of heads. Or, white pugrees to be precise. It was meant to be a student's rally but Tikait had usurped the show. Dressed in white kurta-pyjamas and pugrees, the older Jats looked burly and benevolent as they sat in circles smoking hukkahs. The younger lot carried well-oiled sticks, itching to find a suitable backside. It didn't matter to them that the anti-reservation students were actually on their side. After all, the Jats too, were at the receiving end of the Mandal stick. These guys just wanted a brawl. It was a sort of release for them. When they couldn't find anyone to fight against, they started breaking streetlamps, twisting iron gates and breaking the windows of the DTC buses passing by. Mayhem seemed to be their idea of merriment.

Mastana, Anirban and others stood below a tree watching the action. A couple of anti-Mandal JNU professors were also there. They were visibly taken aback by the rowdyism. Some of them admitted to be first-timers at a political rally of this nature. They had discovered that there was a major difference between political theory and mass agitational politics, at least of this variety.

Anirban wanted to go back but Mastana said it was better to hang about. They sat down under the shade of some trees, waiting for the speeches to be over. Nobody could hear clearly what was being said as the dozens of loudspeakers cancelled each other out. But the general tone was that the government must change its policy.

Some student leaders from Delhi University had also gathered there. 'I think we should try to contact all the top United Front leaders and ask for a little concession,' one of them said.

'For what?' someone asked.

'We should ask for five attempts for every civil services candidate and that the age limit should be increased to 30.'

'Will they agree?' another student asked.

'We should try. We should immediately form a committee of students who will meet them. We should find out who knows whom. They know we are angry. At this moment, they will do anything to calm us. For them, this will be a small concession,' Mastana said.

'I agree. Actually some students have already formed a core committee in the Ramjas hostel. If you are interested, you can join us. Where are you from?' asked a student, who looked like a leader.

'JNU.'

'Achcha! We had heard that most of JNU is pro-Mandal.'

'No. Some students are, some aren't.'

It was decided that whoever was interested should meet outside Haryana leader Devi Lal's home at 8 a.m. the following day.

On the way back, Mastana was far more cheerful than usual. He seemed to harbour a secret desire to be a student leader. 'Come to my room around 7.30 a.m. tomorrow,' Mastana said.

Anirban nodded vaguely. He knew he wouldn't be going again.

25

The caste of love

THE ANTI-MANDAL MOVEMENT had worked hugely in favour of lovers in the campus. During such periods of intense agitation, rules were generally relaxed. Girls could come in and go out of the boys' hostel much more freely.

That evening, Anirban was lying naked on the floor of his room. He was about to get dressed when Purnima, who was drawing rings around his left nipple, said, 'Do you know that I am an OBC?'

A couple of grenades exploded in Anirban's brain.

'No. I didn't. But then I was never interested in caste,' he said, with the poise and calm of an iceberg.

'Well, now you know. I am a Koeri. My grandfather grew vegetables. My father was the first person to go to college in my family. And I am the first girl to do so. And now that you have been sleeping with an OBC girl, I want to know your views on Mandal. Are you for or against reservations for OBCs?'

'I don't know, Purnima,' Anirban replied with his trademark caution. 'I know that OBCs deserve some kind of pro-active help in education. I also know they are educationally backward and need state support. But 27 per cent reservations? Isn't that too much? What would be left for people like us?'

'50.5 per cent. Isn't that enough for you guys?'

'No. The competition is too much.'

'Well. It won't be easy, I accept that. But India needs something as radical as this. V.P. Singh has shown incredible guts in doing what he has done for us disadvantaged communities. I think it will change the politics of the country for ever,' Purnima said.

'Well, he has certainly changed our lives,' Anirban said sarcastically, but without any overt sarcasm in his voice.

'So what happens to us?' Purnima asked. She was now sitting in a corner smoking a Wills Light.

'What do you mean?' he said.

'Are we in a relationship? And is it going to be affected?' she asked.

'I never knew we were in a relationship. You are the one who had said you didn't want a relationship with anybody. So I thought we were just friends having fun. Now you are linking all this with Mandal. Where is the connection?' he asked.

It wasn't exactly a question; more an observation.

'There is a connection and, a very clear one. Mandal is an important step towards achieving social justice. It is a very, very important thing for every OBC like me.'

'It must be. But why are you suddenly making it important for us?' Anirban was genuinely perplexed.

'I hope you know that I have quit the Free Thinkers. I cannot handle your party's—we oppose the Mandal Commission in toto—stand. And I have realized these past few days eating in the hostel mess, how much caste still matters in our society. You know, these girls from Stephen's, LSR, Miranda House and IT College, Lucknow, they are as casteist as anybody else. Such bitches! No one can see Mandal as a progressive step.'

'Look, Purnima, I am not a political person. And as you know, I don't have strong views on anything. Maybe I am wrong. Maybe I will have a different view later. But right now, I feel that Mandal hasn't been implemented the right way. It is going to affect the future of a generation of students like us.'

'But it is also going to change the lives for the better for many. For many who are historically disadvantaged. Can't you see that?'

'I can. But I cannot get myself to be on that side at the moment. I will be dishonest to myself if I say I do.'

'And I will be dishonest to myself if I say that I enjoy fucking a guy whose views are not progressive, politically.'

'You are making things difficult for us.'

'I am just taking an honest stand,' Purnima said. She had finished her cigarette by now.

Anirban waited for her to get up. Strangely, she didn't. For a long time. Maybe because Purnima knew that once she stepped out of the room, she wouldn't be coming back soon.

And when she finally left, Anirban felt with dread that she wasn't coming back ever.

26

The love story of Bhatia

BHATIA WAS SLEEPING with his manhood shamelessly peeping out of his underpants. This was new. Generally, he offered a glimpse of his butt cleavage as he slept through the mornings. Anirban knew his roommate would rather miss his bath and breakfast than a late night tryst with Svetlana. On some nights before going to sleep, Bhatia would request him to get his breakfast. If he wasn't in a real hurry, Anirban would.

People are blinded by love. Bhatia had turned deaf as well. He was oblivious to the anti-Mandal agitation. He continued to spend every evening and much of the night with Ms Pashkova somewhere in the sprawling campus.

Making out in the open air was one of the not-so-secret pleasures of JNU. You could beat about the bush, literally. But (nature) lovers also faced a host of perils that weren't easily explainable to a doctor.

Bhatia once narrated something strange to Anirban. 'We were sitting by the rocks one night when I saw a snake slithering towards us. It was just five yards away and too late to run. I didn't want to startle either Svetlana or the snake. So I just froze. Would you believe it, the snake went right over my feet. I was like stone cold and shivering. O God, that was real close,' he said.

The incident had occurred a few days after anti-Mandal students were out on the streets tearing down public and private property in various towns and kasbas of north India.

Anirban didn't know how to snub Bhatia. He felt like telling his roomie, 'Delhi is burning and all you've got to say is how a snake went over your feet?' But as usual, he couldn't get himself to say what he wanted to. 'You have to be careful in future. By the way, the Mandal thing has spread fast,' is all Anirban said.

'Oh,' Bhatia muttered, kicked off his chappals, picked up his headphones and shut out the world. He was a self-contained unit, happy with his girl and beer, in that order. Like an innocent tribal living in the back of beyond, he seemed untouched by and indifferent to the larger world. What could you say of a guy who had spent four semesters without attending a single demonstration or even casting his vote once?

On a night when he had drunk like a fish, Bhatia confessed to Anirban that he was in love with another woman. 'You know, Anirban, I am totally torn between two women. I have realized I love both Sunita and Svetlana,' said Bhatia.

Nikhil-ji had surprised Anirban. This shocked him. For all his faults, Bhatia appeared to be the one-woman type of man and totally devoted to Svetlana. Or so he thought. Well, he was wrong.

'Boss, I always thought there is only Svetlana in your life. I have never heard you talk or discuss anybody by the name of Sunita. Who is she?'

'She is a third year student in Spanish. Her father is a lecturer in Hissar,' Bhatia said.

'But JNU is a small place. Almost like a village. How could you hide the fact that you are two-timing the girls? Don't they know?'

'Please don't use the word "two-timing". I love both of them. Yesterday, someone told me that Federico Fellini had once said, it is possible to be in love with two, even three women, at a time,' Anirban's roomie replied.

What he actually should have said is, can I have my cake and eat it too? Anirban thought. Aloud he said, 'But how did you manage to keep it a secret?'

'Well, Sunita isn't a hosteller. She stays with her local guardian in South Extension. And Svetlana doesn't have too many friends. Most students she speaks with are fellow Russians,' Bhatia could barely suppress a smug smile.

Svetlana had grown up in the small town of Chadan in the USSR. Her father was a coalminer. In the local community hall, he had watched Raj Kapoor's *Awara* more than half a dozen times. Like many Russians of his generation, he was in love with the movie, its protagonist and its title song. In her childhood days, Svetlana had displayed an extraordinary felicity for the language.

The best students of her school were sent to a language college in Moscow and she was the only one from her class. Thanks to her wonderful Hindi teacher, who had spent several years in Delhi and Benaras in the late 1970s, she too, fell in love with Premchand. In her college, she was again one of the toppers. A trip to JNU was part of the reward. Gaining fluency in the language was her field trip exercise.

'But don't you feel guilty? How would you feel if one of the girls did the same thing to you?' Anirban asked him.

'That's the problem. I don't even feel a twinge of guilt, I swear. When I meet Sunita in the afternoon, I feel I love her. And, obviously, when I meet Svetlana in the night, I know I love her too. Believe me, it is possible to love two women at a time, even three. Mark my words, one day you will feel the same thing. Boss, that guy Fellini wasn't bullshitting. He is a great filmmaker and must have felt something deep to say something like that.'

'So what is your problem then?'

'My problem is how to keep it a secret. I want both of them as long as I can.'

'And what would you do when it is out in the open?'

'I don't know.'

Over the next few weeks, Bhatia seemed to settle down to a convenient routine. Sunita by day and Svetlana by night—life was 'two good' for him.

But very few escape comeuppance.

Sunita came to know, through a common friend of course, what Bhatia had been up to. She confronted him the next morning. Bhatia admitted to his crime and misdemeanour. He was counting on the fact that being a girl from a conservative family, she wouldn't like to spill the beans on anybody.

He was wrong. Sunita bared her broken heart and the extent of its pain, one learnt later, to a cousin, who in turn, immediately relayed the news to her brother. Soon, her newly revealed love-life became a matter of family honour. The girl, obviously, was sharply rebuked but it was the bastard who needed to be taught a lesson.

Bhatia was sipping a glass of chiku shake at a juice parlour in Munirka, when a bunch of beefy Jats accosted him. They seemed to have done their homework well for they did not even ask him his name or anything. Barring showering abuses that involved the private parts of Bhatia's sister, mother, even grandmother, they let their hands and a hockey stick do most of the talking. The assault was fast and furious. By the time, the Jat justice league had delivered its verdict, Bhatia was begging for mercy. Even the normally couldn't-care-less Delhi crowd of casual onlookers was pleading with them to stop.

The beating was carried out both to humiliate and hurt him. The brothers-in-arms could have killed Bhatia if they wanted to. A couple of bones in his left hand needed repairs but he was bruised all over, the flesh tenderized like marinated meat. Bhatia's hand was put in a cast at the JNU hospital. He was given a shot of painkillers and advised to rest for the next couple of weeks.

When Bhatia reached his room Anirban was writing a term paper. '*Kuchh mat pooch yaar abhi. Baat karne se bhi bahut dard hota hai*,' he mumbled, indicating his reluctance to talk about the incident and plonked down on the bed.

But Anirban couldn't help asking, '*Par hua kya*…what happened, yaar?'

'Sunita's brothers,' is all he said. The rest was left unsaid but immediately understood. Friends always do.

Around 8 p.m., Bhatia was nibbling at a soup stick that Anirban had brought for him, when there was a soft knock on the back door.

Bhatia knew who it was. He would probably have run faster than Carl Lewis, if he could. In reality, he was completely immobile, like a swaddled baby. Anirban opened the door. Of course, it was Svetlana.

It wasn't every day that a JNU student is roughed up in Munirka or anywhere else and turned into a rag doll. The incident was the campus gossip of the day and spiced up with every fresh narrative. When someone told Svetlana that the person at the receiving end was none other than her boyfriend, she almost fainted in disbelief. When she saw her boyfriend in such a pathetic state—hand in cast, bandages all over—tears involuntarily swelled up her large eyes.

'Oh my God,' she kept repeating like a parrot.

Anirban got up to leave the room. He wanted the two to be alone for some time. Thrash things out. But Bhatia asked him to stay on. For him, it was confession time. And so, perhaps for the first time in his life, truth poured out like puke from Bhatia. It was purgatory. Anirban wasn't sure how Svetlana was reacting. He couldn't see her face. She was quiet, listening to everything, letting everything sink in. It was a masterclass in the art of pleading for mercy. When it was all over, she quietly got up and left.

'It's all over,' Bhatia groaned. 'I have lost both of them.'

As usual he was wrong. Svetlana returned an hour later with some chicken broth done the Russian way and buttered toast. For the next fortnight or so she visited him twice every day, feeding him chicken stew and bread. She nursed him back to health.

27

Going home, again

EVERYBODY WAS SHOCKED TO discover that Anirban had scored an overall B plus at the end of four semesters.

One of the faculty members, who didn't like him much, actually told him, 'I can see you have improved dramatically. Keep working hard, stay focused and you will be fine.'

That made his day.

He had to surrender the hostel room in a few days. His future plan was simple: Clear the MPhil test, get readmitted to JNU, get the new hostel room and prepare for the civil services. All four attempts, if need be, no thanks to the MCR.

He was not sure if his parents could fund him any further. But Anirban didn't see that as a hurdle. He was keen to take tuitions or work part-time in a newspaper to arrange the money. Whatever it took.

Like most small-town boys, he had at first resisted Delhi. But the city had gradually seduced him. He hadn't achieved much in JNU. But at least he had acquired the confidence to negotiate life. That was enough.

But before that he wanted to go home. Once.

As usual, the journey on the Hatia–Amritsar express was an exercise in masochism. It was an express train that behaved like a local, stopping at railway stations where nobody got off or came aboard. Anirban remembered the three stations named after British civil servants—Robertsonganj, Wyndhamganj, Daltonganj. There was a fourth place too. Mcluskieganj, built as a home and haven for Anglo-Indians. Now the place had fallen through the cracks, a ghost town haunted by a past nobody cared for.

Travelling over the years, he had seen how the trees had vanished from the Jharkhand forests through which the trains made their way. It was a tragedy nobody seemed to be interested in.

Anirban got off at Rampur, an army cantonment that had sprung into national consciousness after a bunch of Sikh recruits killed the unit's brigadier in revolt after the 1984 riots. They had set off for the national capital but were intercepted midway.

The train would have taken another four hours to reach Ranchi. But you could get off at Rampur, take a bus or van and reach home in an hour. He took a bus, sitting on top of it along with some locals who were going to the city to sell kaind, a local fruit, bright yellow in colour. He bought some and started unpeeling and eating them. Sitting on the roof, he felt a little unsafe but far more free.

On two occasions, Anirban had had a narrow escape. The first time, he was saved by a fellow passenger who foresaw the danger as the branch of a tree came perilously close to sweeping him off the roof. The second time, an old tribal spotted an electricity wire dangling ahead. He screamed so loud that the driver immediately applied the brakes to avoid the mishap. Moments after the possible disaster, everyone was back to being normal. It was as if nothing had happened.

Anirban was shocked to see his father. He had aged much beyond his years. His mother told him that he had been unwell for weeks and refused to see a doctor. 'He coughs all night. When I ask him to go for a check-up, he says he's feeling better. But he has lost all energy. He is too weak to even work in the kitchen garden,' his mother was talking and crying.

Yet, strangely, Anirban did not feel the helplessness that swept over him in such moments. Maybe he had really grown up in JNU. It had nothing to do with fighting an election or being dumped by a girl or getting decent grades. It was just that after some time, for no reason other than the reason itself, everybody grows up. Of course, what we grow up into depends a lot on what we read and the company we keep. Maybe the campus—the words and the ideas that floated in its free air—had changed him.

Which is why, even though he could sense everything around him getting darker, Anirban was clear about what he needed to do. He told his father that he would take him to the doctor the next day. And he did. The doctor examined him for a long, long time. He wrote out a prescription and asked for a blood and sputum test. When he went back to the doctor with the reports, two days later, he wrote out some more medicines. 'It's not what I was suspecting. It's a serious lung infection but the antibiotic should do the job,' he said.

It was a small thing but Anirban realized that, for the first time, he had taken his father to the doctor and not the other way around.

His father improved in a few days. Anirban spent the days reading classics borrowed from the nearby Ramakrishna Mission library. Thomas Hardy's *Far from the Madding Crowd*, Somerset Maugham's *Of Human Bondage* and Charles Dickens's *A Tale of Two Cities*.

But the book that really drew him into its own world was Nirmal Verma's *Ve Din*, a story of hesitant love between an Indian student and a German woman set in Prague.

He met his old friends, of course. When they asked him uncomfortable questions such as '*What about UPSC?*' he had a simple and steady answer: 'Haven't started preparing seriously yet. But plan to begin soon.' Even though the look on their faces said *So what were you fucking about in the past two years?* he didn't feel compelled to answer them.

By the time it was time for him to leave a fortnight later, his father had recovered. He was sitting in the backyard under the mango tree when Anirban walked up to him. He knew that his son was leaving—and it seemed to make him sad.

'You don't have to send me money for more than six months. I will manage after that,' Anirban said.

'How?'

'I will appear for the UGC scholarship tests. And I will be taking tuitions.'

'Oh,' is all his father said.

Anirban slept his way back in the upper berth. He dreamt of nothing.

28

A surprise

BACK IN THE campus, Anirban was coming back from Ganga dhaba when he saw a familiar figure walking towards him. He could recognize that gait from a mile. It was Geetha Kasturi.

'Hi,' Anirban said.

'Going back to the hostel?' she asked.

'Yes.' He was keeping it short.

'Can I take you out for dinner tonight?'

'Surprised' isn't the right word. He was knocked out. They hadn't met in weeks, maybe months.

'We haven't met in ages,' she said.

While that was true, it is equally true that we always manage to meet those whom we really want to meet.

Ever since he had become friends with benefits with Purnima, Anirban had convinced himself that Geetha wasn't the kind of woman he wanted. In any case, she was going steady with someone else.

It had been weeks since he had that Mandal conversation with Purnima. In his dreams, he had tried many times to talk to her. In real life too, he tried a couple of times. Once he stood outside her hostel and sent word in, as was the normal practice. The messenger came back saying she was busy and would talk to him when free. She never did.

At the moment, Geetha Kasturi's evening offer looked like a nice escapade.

'Where and what time?' he asked.

'Meet me at 7, at Ganga bus stop. I won't tell you where we are going. The place is a surprise,' she said.

'Let it be a nice one,' he joked.

'Depends,' she said slyly and was gone.

Anirban wanted to shower. But the taps were dry till 7 and he hadn't saved a bucket that day. He washed his face and splashed himself generously with Bhatia's Old Spice cologne. He was waiting for Geetha at the bus stop when he spotted the most ubiquitous guy on the campus.

He was tall and middle-aged. A salt-and-pepper beard was his signature. And he had an awkward walk that reminded one of the Hollywood cowboys of the 1950s. Everybody knew who he was—a sub-inspector from the Intelligence Bureau who was all eyes and ears for any politically subversive activity in the campus. IB guys are meant to be shadows. This guy was like a well-known monument; he was so famous and conspicuous that he had become a standing joke. The IB man was talking to a hostel karamchari who was unsuccessfully trying to fend him off.

'Hi! What are you staring at?' Geetha had arrived. One look at the IB guy and she exhaled, 'Oh!'

In a dark red salwar-kurta, she looked dressed for the occasion.

'So where are we going? Is it Sona Rupa?' The no-fuss tandoori chicken restaurant near AIIMS was a favourite of JNU students.

'Think something classier,' she said.

They took the 615. Near Sarojini Nagar, they got separate seats. The slim Sardarji sitting next to him got down at National Archives. Anirban gestured to Ms Kasturi to come over and sit by his side. Their bodies brushed against each other as the bus swerved in the roundabouts.

'We are going to Nirula's Chinese Room in the outer circle,' she finally revealed the venue. They requested the driver to stop before the bus turned towards Minto Road.

Anirban was pleasantly surprised by the Chinese Room. It was simply the classiest restaurant he had ever been to. Geetha appeared to know what to order. Anirban was quietly ecstatic when he heard her asking for two bottles of beer.

And then, for the first time, he noticed a hint of make-up on her face. Anirban felt like commenting on this extremely nuanced development but restrained himself. It had been a mildly pleasing evening thus far. He didn't want to spoil it.

'How serious are you about Purnima?'

The question seemed to be carefully casual. But it had come out of the blue and Anirban was struck by the bolt. Silence is a superb option in such awkward situations. But it wasn't of much help here. They were sitting in a largely empty restaurant.

'I don't know,' he said.

It was an honest answer. But to someone unaware of the relationship's internal dynamics, it felt like fibbing.

'Really?' she was sarcastic.

'Yes, really,' he said, softly but firmly. 'And I want you to know that I am not being secretive. It is the truth.'

'Okay, if you say so. I won't push you,' she replied, not entirely willing to believe him.

There was a clumsy silence for a minute or two. Thankfully, the waiter arrived with the green bottles of Dansberg beer and poured it into two mugs.

'Cheers,' she said.

'Is that a photograph of Kanchenjunga?' asked Anirban, pointing towards a snow-submerged peak in a photo frame.

She looked hard and said, 'Can't make out. Why did you say that? How's it different from Everest or K2?'

'I don't know. But I can always recognize Kanchenjunga,' he said.

And then, as it often happens with footloose conversations, it veered from Kanchenjunga, the mountain peak, to *Kanchenjunga*, the film. Geetha said the film was 'too bourgeois' for her liking, and Anirban countered that would be entirely missing the point. He pointed out that the film's narrative structure was both innovative and fluid and the way Ray handled class differences and the greys in a relationship made it a movie ahead of its time.

'Even I don't know where my relationship with Srinivas is headed for,' she suddenly burst out.

Has the beverage made her tipsy? Anirban wondered. This again was out of the blue and he didn't quite know what to say.

Silence would have surely been construed as being rude. He felt both sympathetic and curious. He carefully processed his response in the next few seconds.

'I am so sorry. I hope it is nothing major,' he said, without really meaning it.

'It is. Next month he is going to Chicago for his PhD. Where does that leave us?'

'Well, if a relationship is strong, that's a non-issue. I think you are over-worrying.'

'We have had major fights recently. He doesn't want to get married now. And I don't want to push him. So there are no guarantees about what will happen next.'

'There are no guarantees in marriage too. What matters is commitment.'

'I have doubts on that count too.'

The waiter had arrived to ask if they wanted another bottle and she said, yes.

'And it isn't just that,' she seemed to be letting her guard down.

'Actually, I think he isn't serious about the relationship anymore. I think he is moving away from me and has no intentions of looking back.'

'What makes you think so negatively? Maybe he is just a little anxious. You just need to soothe his nerves a bit. As I said, you are probably being just a little too overeager.'

She baulked at the word. 'Overeager? Me? Of course not! But I can feel it in my bones that we might be going separate ways eventually.'

The main course arrived. They ate quietly. Anirban

liked the Szechuan chicken. After dinner, they went for ice cream downstairs.

'Will you drop me home in an auto?' Geetha asked him suddenly. She sounded a wee bit tipsy.

'Of course,' he said. 'Where do your parents live?'

'In RK Puram, near Sangam Cinema,' she said.

As they took the ride back, Anirban felt the early winter breeze on his face. After those two bottles of beer and plenty of true confessions, Geetha had turned reticent. And Anirban felt he should just let her be.

The auto was about to enter the colony when Geetha asked the driver to stop. She paid him off. Anirban had thought he would be taking the same auto to JNU but she had different ideas. 'It's not too late. You will get an auto or a bus any time. Just walk me home. It is less than half a kilometre away.'

The area was ill-lit. Most street lights were off. And the shadows of trees ensured that the road was dark. *Just the ideal venue for a chain snatcher*, Anirban thought. In this sarkari colony, everybody seemed to be home watching DD. It was Wednesday and this was *Chitrahaar* time.

As they were crossing a particularly shaded area, Anirban could feel Geetha take his hand in hers. An unnameable thrill surged through him from head to heels. *God, is this really happening?* Anirban asked himself. The next moment, she had wrapped her arms around his waist. And then he found himself at the receiving end of a ferocious liplock. It was less a kiss, and more an assault. He felt crushed by its aggression and the overwhelming pleasure it brought.

He kissed her back—and when he found her tongue, he sucked at it so hard that it was in serious danger of being uprooted.

Where do fear and shame and everything else that stops us from doing these things out in the open vanish on such occasions? Anirban couldn't help wondering, even as he started kissing her in other places. Soon, she was making the sort of noises you generally heard in a Donna Summers album.

They stopped abruptly at the sound of an approaching Ambassador. By the time the car passed, so had the moment of madness. For a few seconds they kept staring at each other. To continue or not to continue, that seemed to be the question. This time Anirban held her hand and led her to a tree by the road. He pushed her against its trunk, squashing her breasts in the process, and kissed her again.

'I think I should go home now,' she said, 'We cannot finish here what we started.'

'No, we can't,' Anirban said.

Probably, she was expecting him to say more.

Some months back, he might have said a lot more. But Anirban was past those days of innocence and effusiveness. All he said was, 'Can I walk with you a little further?'

'Fine,' she said.

After another 50 yards or so, she pointed her hand towards a white Maruti parked by the road. 'Can you see that car? My flat is just a two-minute walk from there.'

'Well, good night then,' Anirban said.

Walking back, the enormity of the evening dawned on

Anirban. He wanted to pinch himself to find out if what had happened had really occurred. He had no idea what it really meant and what its long-term after-effects were going to be. He knew he was swept away. He knew that she was vulnerable. It was the beer too. But he couldn't help feeling curiously elated and elevated with what had happened. His head was spinning like a weathercock in the wind.

There are many theories on relationships, even those which are half, incomplete. Some relationships take time to reach the next level because we don't realize its true potential. You gradually warm up to them. *Is this one of them*, Anirban wondered?

Suddenly, he saw he was actually nearing the Munirka bus stop. He had walked over two kilometres without even realizing it. Thankfully, the 615 didn't make him wait long. For once, he could spot a couple of vacant seats. The bus was full of JNU students who were talking animatedly about *Reds*, the Warren Beatty film they had seen at Chanakya.

On his way back to the hostel, he saw Purnima talking to the presswala at the Nilgiri dhaba. He knew she hadn't seen him. And he knew that even if she had, she would not call out. His mind was muddled with the after-taste of what had happened an hour ago. He didn't know how the future would pan out with either of the two girls. And actually, he wasn't in any hurry to find out.

29

A train journey

A WEEK PASSED by aimlessly, making Anirban feel almost like a vagabond. Strangely, after that eventful evening, he never saw Ms Kasturi in the campus. He wished that she would call on him but it never happened.

It was a late Sunday morning and Anirban was drinking coffee in the common room, which was fairly empty. Some months back it had been entirely different, when an overwhelming majority of hostellers would be watching *Mahabharat* sipping tea from their stainless steel glasses. Even those studying for the civil services would spare time for the serial as if not watching it would invite the wrath of the gods. For once, JNU was in tune with the rest of India. But *Mahabharat* had run its course. The hostel seemed indifferent to the new serial.

Suddenly Anirban saw Mastana beckoning him from the door.

'Hello!' Mastana was unusually grave.

'Hello,' Anirban mumbled. '*Kya baat hai?*'

'Do you know that Purnima's daughter is down with a

strange fever? She's seriously ill and has been admitted to some private hospital in Arrah. I am told Purnima left for home by the evening train yesterday.'

Mastana was one of the few guys Anirban had confided in. He knew how and why his friendship with Purnima had unscrambled.

A short film of moments spent with Purnima flashed before him. She would often speak to him about her daughter. He knew that a fierce desire to give her a good life is what spurred her. Dori was her stimulus, her world.

Suddenly Anirban felt he should be there by Purnima's side in her moment of real need. The backlog of term papers, the looming semester tests, the civil services project—nothing seemed to matter. He was swamped by a restless desire to be with her. He remembered what Sahir Ludhianvi had once written about love. *Ishq bechain khayalon ke siva kucch bhi nahi.* Love is nothing but restless thoughts. Now he understood what it actually meant.

Money was a problem. But Anirban felt no shame in borrowing for the girl (and he was beginning to admit this to himself) he really cared for. It is probably during such unexpected moments when you realize what a person really means to you. It hurt him that she was upset. He wanted to make things better for her.

Thankfully, he didn't have to beg around for the cash. The first person he went to, Nikhilji, didn't even ask him why he wanted the money. He reached out for the drawer in the study table, took out his wallet and handed him Rs 1000.

Anirban knew it was no use trying to reserve a seat at such a short notice. The touts ensured that. He grabbed a regular ticket and slipped into an evening train to Patna.

The unreserved second-class compartment had enough people to fill a small stadium. Most of them were marginalized men from the hinterland, joyous labourers going back home. Almost all of them were carrying hard-earned cash toiling in the wheat fields of Punjab. Often they would subconsciously touch the pockets of their pants to check and assure themselves that it was still there. They were sharing everything. Food, tea, khaini, jokes. They knew how to share, probably because that's what life had taught them to do.

In the compartment, they were also sharing space. The upper berth had four grown-up men curled up like prawns. Every berth had at least three or four people sitting on them. Anirban found some room on the floor close to the bathroom door. The reason why it was still unoccupied soon became clear to him. It blocked the way to the loo. Every time somebody wanted to ease his bladder or bowel movements, he had to make adjustments. Then there was the unyielding stench of urine, the signature of every loo in second-class compartments. Luckily, after three hours of coping with this pitiless onslaught on his olfactory organs, Anirban found some space away from the loo. He held his backpack in his hand, curled up in a foetal position and tried to sleep. Rather strangely, he succeeded. It wasn't deep sleep; more a sort of drifting in and out of slumber. He woke up with a start around 7 just when the train was entering Patna station.

Anirban got down from the express train and switched platforms to take a morning local to Arrah. He had taken Purnima's home address from her roommate. Anirban wasn't sure whether she would be at home or in the hospital. In any case, he had no idea which hospital she would be in. So he took a rickshaw to her home near Pakdi Chowk.

He was aware that Arrah was an extremely conservative town. And he wasn't exactly sure about the kind of reception he would get. The truth was that Purnima was only separated from her husband. The divorce had never happened. She hadn't asked for it and he never bothered about it. But he had married again—and was father to a bonny boy, Purnima had told him once. And, yes, he didn't spare a single paisa for his daughter's upkeep.

Anirban asked the rickshawala to wait as he knocked at the door. Thankfully, there were no neighbours ogling nearby.

An elderly woman opened the door. Anirban could only say that he was Purnima's classmate from JNU and had come to visit her.

She looked surprised but managed to mumble that both Purnima and her father were at Meera Nursing Home near Moti Mahal Cinema. He didn't know what more to say as he took her leave.

The rickshawala hadn't heard of Meera Nursing Home but took him to Moti Mahal. Anirban went to a paan shop near the cinema hall and enquired about the private hospital. The guy at the counter just craned his neck towards the left.

Sporting a huge, red signboard, the nursing home stood out in a crop of unremarkable double-storey buildings. A ward boy of sorts sat in a corner near the reception. Anirban asked him about the ICU and he pointed to the staircase leading to the second floor.

He got lucky. The moment he stepped on the second floor, Anirban saw Purnima walking towards him, holding a piece of paper in hand. The paper, Anirban noticed as she came closer, was a prescription.

She looked at him as if she had been expecting him.

He spoke to her as if they had never fought.

'How's she now?' he asked.

'Don't know. Doctors are not sure if she will pull through,' she said. Her voice was remarkably poised for a grieving mother. Maybe calamity calms you in a strange way.

Then, as an immediate afterthought, she asked, 'Who told you about this?' 'Mastana,' he replied. And then, taking care not to make it sound like an accusation, he complained, 'You should have told me about this before you left.'

She replied with silence. They were walking down the stairs now. Soon, they were out of the hospital and walking towards the medicine shop flanking its left side.

'She is on an intravenous drip. Got to buy a couple of saline water bottles,' she said.

'What exactly is wrong with Dori?' he asked.

'Have you heard of Japanese Encephalitis?'

He nodded vaguely.

'It is caused by mosquito bites. Hundreds die of encephalitis every year in Bihar and UP.'

'Why? Is there no cure?'

'No. The treatment is only for symptomatic relief. You get splitting headaches, high fever and a stiff neck. Sometimes you get convulsions. I am told it also affects the brain.

'Oh! How is she responding so far?'

'We will know in a couple of days.'

Anirban could see Purnima was trying extra-hard to behave normal. They took the bottles and walked back to the ICU, which was buzzing with more personal attendants than nurses. *What kind of an ICU is this?* Anirban thought. And this was supposed to be one of the better private hospitals in town.

Dori was fast asleep. Purnima handed over the bottles to a nurse, who kept staring at Anirban for some reason. A gentleman with incredibly sad eyes was sitting by one of the beds. 'This is my father,' she said. Anirban folded his hands to greet him. He shook his head but didn't say anything. Purnima did not introduce him to her father.

Instead she said, 'All the four beds here are occupied by encephalitis patients. It is an epidemic of sorts. See Arrah is less than 60 kilometres from Patna but it still doesn't make the front page of even local newspapers like *The Indian Nation*.'

They stood next to her father for about 10 minutes. Neither of them spoke. Then Purnima slowly started walking out of the ICU. 'I will be back in a few minutes,' she told her father.

They stopped at a roadside teashop just outside the hospital. It's strange how all hospitals, courts and government offices prompt the same kind of support industry nationwide, Anirban observed. Purnima ordered lemon tea and they stood awkwardly below a tree as onlookers gaped at them. They seemed to be figuring out the nature of the relationship between the two. Anirban didn't care, and it seemed, neither did Purnima.

'Why are you here?' she asked.

'Because I want to be with you.'

'Now that you are here, what will you do?'

'I don't know. Everything. Anything. I am here to ease your load as much as I can.'

'That is both nice and kind of you. But this is a very conservative place. Where will you stay? You can't stay at my home. And you shouldn't stay in any lodge. Things could get complicated.'

'I don't know anything. I just want to help you.'

'Why?'

'Because I have realized that I love you. I want to live my life with you.'

Now both were silent. She was trying to soak in the weight of his words and find a suitable reply.

Finally, she said, 'I think you should leave. That would be the proper thing to do. I am not saying I don't need your help. But we can manage here. If you stay, there will be gossip in the locality. It will complicate things unneccesarily with my husband. As you know, he has married again. But as far as our marriage is concerned, we are only separated, not divorced. You have got to understand that this is an entirely different world from JNU.'

'But I want to stay!' Anirban protested.

'I know. But you must go.'

'Do you love me?' he asked her.

She didn't reply. She just walked up to the tea seller and paid him a one-rupee coin. Anirban walked alongside her. When they reached the hospital, she said, 'I hate to say this again. But you must go. Bye.'

And Purnima walked away.

On his way to the railway station, Anirban realized that he had travelled 15 hours for a 15-minute conversation.

30

A confession

'How was the trip? Everything okay?' Mastana asked Anirban when the two met during lunch a couple of days later.

'No. Her daughter has got this thing called Japanese Encephalitis. I am told it affects the brain.'

'Japanese Encephalitis is common in some districts of Bihar and eastern UP. Let us pray she pulls through,' Mastana said.

'Yeah.'

'By the way,' he said, 'that SFI girl had come looking for you. She said it is urgent.'

Anirban knew who he was talking about. There was no love lost between the two and Mastana wouldn't even refer to her by her name.

Immediately, a cluster of questions started tickling his brain. *Has she broken off with Srinivas? Does she want a proper relationship with me? How am I going to accept her when I am madly in love with Purnima?* The evening spent with Ms Kasturi at Nirula's Chinese Room and everything that had occurred thereafter flashed like a film before his eyes. So did every possibility.

He was expecting to see her in the library, but Anirban found her in the School of Social Sciences building instead. Geetha Kasturi looked more relieved than happy at seeing him.

'Why are you avoiding me? I went to your hostel twice, looking for you,' she said.

'I was out of town.'

'Really? What happened?'

'It's a long story. Why were you looking for me?' He wasn't sure what tone to adopt.

'Let's go to the library canteen. Tell me the long story as we walk there,' she said.

'Some other time. It won't get over by then,' Anirban resisted.

It was very crowded inside the canteen. Geetha paid for the coffee. They took their cups and sat outside the canteen on the rocks.

'You know, Anirban,' she was trying to control the excitement in her voice, 'Srini and I are getting married next month. I thought I must share the news with you.'

'Wow!' Anirban exhaled.

He thought he was supposed to feel disappointed, drown in anguish. But the moment never arrived. He felt nothing.

'I guess I was being immature,' Ms Kasturi spoke like an errant schoolgirl. 'I didn't understand the depth of his feelings for me. That's why I felt insecure and ended up kissing you that night. But when he came to me the other day and said, "Let us get married, if that's what you want", I felt so guilty.'

'Did you tell him what happened between us?'

'Of course not. Why should I? There's a theory that you should come clean on everything with the person you love. But I don't think my confession will enrich our relationship in any way. What you don't know, never hurts you. Actually, I went to the hostel specifically to ask you to please never ever discuss that evening with anyone. Ever. Hope you haven't already.'

'Geetha,' Anirban spoke slowly, stressing on every word, 'I am a small-town boy. We may be uncool. But we know how to value a friendship. And we know how to keep a secret.'

She nodded gently in relief. 'I knew I could trust you.'

'So where are you getting married?' Anirban was trying to change the topic.

'Oh, here. At the Guruvayur temple, across the Yamuna in east Delhi. I am inviting you now. You must come,' she said.

'Of course,' Anirban said.

'*No, I wouldn't be comfortable doing that*,' is what he should have said but couldn't.

31

A conundrum

THE GENTLEMAN DRESSED in a spotless white kurta-pyjama spoke with a sense of self-importance. But his shoes were covered with dust.

'Where is Nikhil-ji? I am his father,' he spoke with the same authority that Rehman had in his voice playing the zamindar in *Sahib, Bibi Aur Ghulam*. This was feudalism incarnate, where even a father added the suffix 'ji' to his son's name.

Anirban and Nikhil-ji were no longer neighbours after he had got a single seater. But his father seemed to have found out who he needed to talk to about his whereabouts. 'I have been informed that he has been missing for several days now. You are one of his friends, I am told. You must know something about his whereabouts?'

Anirban kept quiet. He knew that a few days back, Nikhil-ji had gathered courage and told his father on the phone about the girl he had fallen in love with. His father had screamed at him and said something which roughly meant that he would have strangled him then and there if he could. He immediately ordered Nikhil-ji back home. When he found his son wasn't as obedient as he used to be, he flew into a rage. He also flew from Patna to Delhi.

Nikhil-ji had disappeared with the girl. It was clear he had decided to avoid a fully frontal confrontation with his domineering father, at least for the time being. He was in double trouble because the girl's brother had filed an FIR at the Vasant Vihar police station claiming his sister had been kidnapped.

A day later, a police constable came to the hostel and asked a few questions about Nikhil-ji's whereabouts, speaking to his roommate under the watchful eyes of the warden and the hostel president.

The same night, around 1 a.m., Anirban heard a soft knock on the door. It was Nikhil-ji. 'I am sorry for hurrying you like this. Can I get my Rs 1,000 back?' he said. 'I need it badly.'

'I can give you only Rs 500 right now. Is that okay?' Anirban asked.

'Okay,' he replied.

'Do you know your father is here? The cops are also looking out for you,' Anirban said.

'I am aware of everything. *Sab khabar milti rehti hai*,' he said, confirming that he was updated on everything. He wasn't nervous but there was an edge to his voice. Nikhil-ji paused and added, 'Don't worry, he will go away in a few days. I will come back to the hostel then.'

'Where are you staying?'

'With a friend in Noida. Don't worry, we are safe,' he said.

'Are you aware an FIR has been filed against you?'

'Who cares? She is an adult. And we are getting married at the Arya Samaj Mandir in Vasant Vihar on Friday. Would you like to be one of our witnesses?'

'Sure,' Anirban said. For long, he had always wanted to be part of an exciting, brave venture. This was a great chance. 'What time?' he asked.

'Exactly 11 o'clock,' Nikhil-ji said.

And then he was gone.

32

A face-off

POISED AMONG CONDESCENDING bungalows in upscale Vasant Vihar, the unassuming Arya Samaj Mandir stood out like an oddity. The colony was home to the city's swank, sedan people but the temple complex was a compact essay in parsimony.

So was the marriage ceremony, conducted by a frail but sage-looking priest who seemed to have harmonized his life with the mantras he recited. For dozens of young couples, high on love and rebellion but a little hard-up on cash, Arya Samaj Mandir was one of the preferred places to get married. It was quick, cheap and unfussy.

Anirban got ready early, got into a clean pair of jeans and a white shirt. He walked up to Mastana's room and asked for a lift. On learning why, he readily agreed. The two drove out on his bike, its exhaust fumes making a decent contribution in creating the ozone hole.

From a distance, Anirban saw Nikhil-ji huddled with a couple of students outside the temple gate. He had never seen those guys before but they were discussing something pretty animatedly. They were his girlfriend Pragya's friends, he learnt later.

Nikhil-ji greeted them warmly. '*Aur* Mastana-ji *bhi aayein hain. Bahut badhiya,*' he said.

But he looked tense for some reason. *Is it because his father is in the city?* Anirban wondered.

'There is something wrong,' he told Mastana.

'Even I can sense it. Maybe Nikhil-ji is afraid that his father will turn up. Has he gone back to Bihar?'

'I don't know. I only hope he doesn't arrive here. Because he doesn't seem to be the kind of guy who is capable of understanding an alternate point of view.'

Anirban wasn't wrong. Within a few minutes, two white Mark IV Ambassadors screeched to a halt in front of the temple. Six flawless specimens of the medieval male swaggered out of them. Two of them carried double barrel guns. Nikhil-ji's father strode towards his son with purpose.

Nikhil-ji had told Anirban once that as a child, he would often enter the house from the back door to avoid facing his father. Not that his father didn't love him or that he didn't care for his pitashree. This was a classic father–son relationship in a feudal setting. A father spoke to his son through his wife. A son spoke to his father through his mother.

Little had changed even after he moved from school to college. But like hundreds of other students from similar backgrounds, he had seen the power and possibility of alternative truths. He understood now that doing the right thing was what was most important, even if it meant going against your father.

Yet, as his father came close, Nikhil reached out to touch his feet. But the old man moved away—he was coiled with rage.

'You never told me you wanted to marry a girl from another caste,' he said, speaking in Bhojpuri, spitting out every word in anger. He seemed to be a firm believer in the sanctity of caste, in the purity of hierarchies.

'I don't care what caste she belongs to. For me she is just the girl I want to marry,' he replied, unflustered.

One of his father's henchman said, 'Nikhil babu, can't you see your father is really angry. As a son, don't you think that you should follow his orders? Don't forget your family always cares about you.'

But Nikhil-ji seemed to be a transformed person. 'I don't know anything about that. At the moment, I would request you, only one thing. Either you bless us as a couple or please leave.'

Nikhil-ji's father was shaken and stirred by this open defiance. On hearing the commotion, Pragya had also rushed out of the mandir.

The scene was unalloyed Bollywood: a bride in a red wedding sari, a bunch of tough men with guns, and a father–son face-off.

But unlike the formula flicks where the climax either ended with the two lovers giving up their lives fighting against a heartless world or their parents undergoing a change of heart, there was an unlikely twist to the tale.

The priest had called the local police who had arrived promptly. The elderly SHO, who appeared to be knocking on the doors of retirement, wasn't happy at the sight of an insolent young man.

'Apne baap ki kyun nahi sunte ho?' he asked Nikhil-ji. It was the eternal lament of all patriarchs—*Why don't you listen to your father?* He would have made a great sarpanch in a Haryana khap village. Iron words in a velvet fist: that seemed to be his style.

Pragya was aware that her brother had filed an FIR against Nikhil-ji, kidnapping being the normal charge against the groom in such cases. She had brought her matriculation certificate, generally accepted as official proof of a birth date. She looked towards Nikhil-ji and said, 'My brother claims in his FIR that this man has kidnapped me. That is not true. I am an adult and I am here of my own will.'

The SHO scratched his head. Before he could react further, Mastana put him on the backfoot by telling him that the police was interfering in the lives of two consenting adults. For good measure, he also bluffed that a busload of students were on their way to the temple from JNU.

Discretion is often the better part of valour. The SHO immediately turned to Nikhil-ji's father and said, *'Ab ke karenge, tau. Chhora-chhori to baalig hai aur shaadi karna chahte hain?* The SHO's question—'What can you and I do, Uncleji, if these guys are adults and want to get married?'—was certainly a valid one.

The stand-off continued without both sides budging an inch. But Mastana had also called up the DCP (south), a young Bihari officer from Muzaffarpur.

When he arrived in his jeep, along with a bunch of cops, the henchmen immediately went back to the cars. They knew the sight of men with guns didn't exactly lend strength to a delicate case. This was south Delhi, not north Bihar.

After patiently listening to both sides of the story, the DCP was polite but firm, 'Sir, we respect your views. But the law doesn't support you,' he told Nikhil-ji's father. 'We have no option but to let them get married. They are adults, after all.'

Nikhil-ji's father couldn't understand how and why he had become the villain of the piece. But he was smart enough to play by the rules of the game. He just disowned his son immediately and told him he could be dead as far he was concerned—'*Hamara tumhara rishta khatam. Aaj yahin mera beta mar gaya.*'

Then he drove away, leaving behind a bunch of relieved people and a cloud of dust.

33

A goodbye

THE MANDAL FEVER slowly fizzled out. The V.P. Singh government had offered a fourth chance to the general category civil services aspirants and raised the maximum age of taking the examinations from 26 to 28. It was an olive branch and many quietly took it because they had realized by then that the decision on reservations for OBCs was irreversible.

One day, Anirban received a letter from Purnima. 'The fever has gone. Dori is recovering slowly and I am nursing her back to health. More than physical, she needs my emotional support,' she wrote.

She wanted to know about him in general: how he was preparing for the civil services, his schedules—the kind of things neighbours ask out of politeness. The letter lacked intimacy and passion; perhaps it was written more out of obligation than desire.

Anirban wrote back saying he was fine. He asked her when she intended to come back. There was no reply. She had been away for over six weeks now.

Rather surprisingly, he spotted her one afternoon at Kamal Complex. She was haggling with a vegetable vendor. 'Hey!' he said, 'When did you come back? How is Dori?'

She smiled. 'Just a couple of days back. She is fine, has started going to school. It was such a narrow escape,' she shook her head, as if reliving those difficult days.

Anirban was hurt. He felt offended too. He had undertaken a 1,000-kilometre long train journey to visit her and she didn't even bother to call on him after getting back. Was it another case of a boy falling in love with a girl who had no love to give? He felt angry that his heart had let him down.

No love is worth losing self-respect, Anirban told himself.

'So how's everything else?' he asked. You always say something like this when you have nothing to say.

'Everything is fine. *Padhai to abhi shuru bhi nahi kiya…*I don't know when I will be able to start studying again,' she said.

Words were rationed to only a few unavoidable ones. Something had happened to her in Arrah; something that had changed her completely. It was as if future possibilities had been dismissed as an unviable option and the past wiped clean from her memory.

'Okay, see you then. Bye,' she said.

34

A conversation

OVER THE YEARS, Anirban had understood and internalized what Shubhalok and Sharad had told him one evening at the Ganga dhaba. That living in JNU is like being in love in middle-age. The feeling is like a pillow by the bedside which offers constant, undemanding companionship. As in any relationship, there are early bouts of suspicion, hesitation, even resistance. But once you learn to embrace what is on offer, the rewards are unlimited.

As usual, the hostel was more than half empty in the summer holidays. As usual, this is when Anriban loved the campus best. He felt he owned it.

For a fortnight, Anirban followed the same routine. He studied all day, taking only loo and mess-room breaks. Occasionally, around 11 at night, he would walk to the Nilgiri dhaba for a glass of coffee. And sometimes he sleep-walked the empty streets. He had become like his seniors.

One night he was sitting on the bench below the tree in front of the Godavari hostel when he heard someone whisper from behind, 'Hello. I knew it was you.'

It was Purnima.

She was coming back from the library.

'Like you, I am also warming up for the UPSC exams,' she said.

'Who told you what I have been doing?'

'Nobody. I just guessed. Correct me, if I am wrong.'

'No, you are not. But I started some days back,' he said honestly.

'Why have you stopped talking to me?' She was cupping her cheeks between her hands, a familiar pose. It was half-complaint, half-curiosity.

'That's very smart. If you remember, I had travelled 1,000 kilometres to meet you in Arrah. I had proposed to you. You turned me away. Then again, we met some months back at Kamal Complex. You seemed totally disinterested. Now you are the one with the grudge. That's a good one.'

For a moment, she was forced into silence by the barrage of accusations. Then she reacted, slowly but clearly, 'I am sorry about that. My mind was not right then. First, it was Dori's illness. Or its after-effects. Then, there was too much of course work.'

'I can understand Dori's illness. But that happened some time back. What about after that? When you give such lame and tame explanations for not meeting a person you once met three times a day, then it means only one thing: you don't miss him. And it means something is missing from the relationship...what's the word, is it passion or urge, or is it both?'

'I am just saying I am sorry for all that happened. Can we be friends again?'

'What kind of friends?'

'The way we used to be.'

'I doubt it. I would be lying if I say that I was not hurt when you refused me point blank. It took a lot to say: I love you. But you refused me for whatever reason. It is not possible, at least for me, to go back to being friends with you. Not in the way we used to be. Even after your refusal, I waited months for you. I had hoped that you would change your mind. It is not ego. But I have decided to put my past behind. I have decided to move on. Life isn't switch on, switch off, Purnima.'

'I never knew you cared so deeply for me.'

'What can I say? I guess either it is my fault that I couldn't make you see that. Or, is it your fault that you didn't want to see it?'

'But, Anirban, we were never meant to be more than friends. So what if we were sleeping with each other? You are the one who shifted the goalposts. And don't forget, your views on Mandal aren't exactly progressive.'

'To begin with, I am beginning to see the merits of Mandal. And that has nothing to do between you and me. I understand now that the case of merit is overstated. That merit could be a cumulation of collective advantages acquired by certain castes over centuries. But what I felt for you had nothing to do with Mandal. And it happened when I got to know that you had left for home to take care of Dori. That's why I travelled to Arrah sitting near the loo in a packed train. But I know you never felt for me that way.'

She was still, her hands cupping her cheeks. Feeling almost sorry for herself, for not being able to reciprocate his ardour.

'I am so sorry I didn't feel about you the same way. For you, our relationship evolved in a certain way. For me, it didn't. But I can't pretend it did. Why don't you understand what I had told you at the very beginning—that I am not ready for the kind of relationship you are looking for. I am too scarred inside,' she said slowly, almost apologetically.

'That's what even I am saying. We don't have to pretend anything anymore. I cannot be friends with you because it would be too harrowing for me. I want to get over you, Purnima.'

'We were once friends and lovers,' she said.

'Of course, if you equate sex with love. Like you, I used to feel that we had such a great arrangement between us. But that arrangement was dismantled by my heart. I cannot rearrange it again. That's why I am telling you again and again: the past is past.'

Anirban continued, 'I am not blaming you for anything. I know what you have been through. I just thought that like me, you might change with time. I also thought that you would have known by now that there are different kinds of men. And that all wounds finally heal, if you give it a chance. Didn't you realize that after all these months? I have now come to believe that you do not want to invest emotionally in a relationship with me. That's the conscious choice you have made.'

'That's not true. Why don't you understand that I can't love anyone, barring my daughter? There's nothing inside me to give. I am an emotional cripple,' she said.

This was the final statement. Stamped. Sealed. Locked. Something snapped inside Anirban.

Sometimes love stories begin and end without real love. Just my bad luck that it turned out to be one of those, Anirban told himself.

~

On his way back, Anirban saw Bhatia walking to his hostel room. They were no longer roommates. Both were enjoying the luxury of single seaters now.

'Hi champion!' Bhatia was warm as ever.

'Hi,' Anirban replied.

'So how's life?'

'Same as usual. Just appeared for the UGC scholarships test two days back and preparing for the civil services,' he said.

'Listen I am going to Chandigarh when the semester ends. And I am taking Svetlana with me. I think it's time my parents, relatives and friends met her. We want to get married next year,' Bhatia was gushing like a teenager.

'Wow! Congrats, man.'

'It will be a real Punjabi wedding. Lots of whisky, bhangra, hot women you can trust. You must come.'

'Of course,' Anirban said.

'I must tell you something more before I leave. I plan to settle down with Svetlana in Moscow. We want to open a restaurant: sell butter chicken, shahi paneer, naan and all that Punjabi stuff. I know these are troubled times out there. Too much political turmoil. But it won't always be so. I want to do this before everybody starts doing it. I have even thought of a name for our restaurant: Disco Chicken. Do you get it? It's from *Disco Dancer*, Mithun's film which is such a superhit in the USSR. What do you think? Great, isn't it?'

'Super,' Anirban said. *Some people are so sorted*, he thought ruefully.

'See you around. By the way, what happened between that Bihari chick and you? She was cool but I don't think she ever loved you.'

'Why do you say that?'

'I never saw any love for you in her eyes. Trust me, I know it when I see it,' Bhatia said.

'You are far more perceptive than I thought,' Anirban conceded.

When Anirban walked into the hostel he could see a group of seniors arguing around the mess table. And when he heard a familiar roar in the common room, he felt reassured that the world hadn't changed.

35

Ten years later

Hi Anirban,

Don't tell me this letter hasn't surprised you. I only hope it is a pleasant one.

I guess it is almost 10 years since we last spoke or met. As I write to you, time snaps back like a rubber band. But let me first tell you what I heard about you from Mastana.

I live in Bombay and I met him the other day at the Marine Lines station. He told me about your father. My condolences. I am sure you must be okay now.

Mastana also told me that you got married a couple of years back. Congrats! How's marriage?

I also know you teach modern Indian history somewhere in Bastar. What went wrong with the civil services? He said you made three attempts, appeared for two interviews. I hope it's not like a dagger in your heart that still hurts. It happens to so many. Remember, life is snakes and ladders. We don't get everything we want.

You might recall that I had suddenly dumped my PhD midway and left for Arrah. But my mamaji, my uncle, changed my life. His sons live in Bombay. They were aware of my interest in art and suggested I come and stay with them.

It is a long story about how I got into the film world. The truth is, their contacts helped me find work as an assistant with Satish Kamath, a well-known art director in Hindi films. After assisting him for three years, I have graduated now to being an art director. If you get a chance, do watch, *Dil aur Dard*. Or *Udhaar ka Sapna*. You can see my name in the opening credits.

It's not something that makes me glow with pride. But I am pretty hopeful that my résumé will look better with time. Just watch out.

What really makes me happy is that Dori is one of the brightest students in her class. That I have my own small flat in Dahesar, a suburb in Bombay, although it isn't easy rustling up Rs 20,000 every month for the instalments. You would be amused to know I made the down payment from the divorce settlement which came through two years back.

I don't know whether you would be interested but I must confide a little about my personal life. I have had a couple of flings here and there. Nothing serious. I still like men though I seem to enjoy masturbation more. Sometimes I fantasize they are your fingers as it often used to be those days. Don't tell me you are not getting a high and a hard-on reading this.

Big confession: Sometimes I think what life with you might have been. Not with a sense of regret but with lots of affection. I can tell you this for sure: After Mama-ji, who helped me find my career and feet in Bombay (or should I say Mumbai?), you are the nicest guy I have ever met. And I know that your love was true and deep.

Don't get me wrong, Anirban. Those days I had my priorities: my daughter and my career. Everything else was irrelevant. I had clarity about that.

The thing is I lost faith in the idea of a marriage or even being in a monogamous live-in relationship. I thought I was scarred for life. Actually, I might still be. But I was wrong about myself on one count. Nobody ever becomes an emotional hollow. We are all capable of love, if we choose to, till the last day of our lives. The heart and the head keep playing games with us. It is just that sometimes we get so twisted that we don't even know ourselves.

Now it doesn't matter. I feel complete. Especially since my daughter is doing so well. I am also addicted to my independence. I hope you understand that it doesn't make me a bad person or a lesser human being.

And I hope you also understand that I am really happy for you. Please think of me as a firm friend forever. Remember you always have a home in Bombay.

Waiting for your reply.

With lots of love.

Purnima.

PS: I miss JNU.

Dear Purnima,

It's been an hour since I finished reading your letter and I am still wrapped up in the emotions it has evoked. I am delighted by some of your confessions. It pampers my ego and penis. Thanks.

On a more serious note, let me first congratulate you on your success and finding happiness. Happiness, I guess, is more elusive. Great to know that so you are so resolved now. I know everything about you revolves around Dori. So I am overjoyed that she is doing so well.

I am not surprised that you have become an art director. For me, you were always an artist. The great thing is that you have found your calling. Not everybody in this world ends up doing the job he or she really wants to do. You are one of the lucky few.

There's a difference between life and livelihood. And that you have been able to fuse the two calls for a celebration. I know you will say things are hardly as rosy as I am making them out to be. What I am saying is, you are on the right track. Bigger and better things await you. Trust me on this.

About me now. You are right, my wife Lily and I teach history in Bastar. It's a clean and quiet life—not the kind I had dreamt of in college but a life without regrets at the same time.

Jagdalpur is a charming little town circled by forests and lakes in the heart of Bastar. I am told it used to be indifferent to change but now the surrounding area is coming under more and more Naxal influence with every passing year. I don't think that's going to change our lives in some significant way. The Reds don't see people like us as part of the problem. We are not exactly what Marx would classify as class enemies.

I have come to love teaching. There is a hunger for learning in these parts. I have realized that students don't want gyan; just guidance. And that's what I do.

Like you, I miss JNU. What I mean is that I miss the JNU of our time; the way it was and the way I remember it. A place is made of people. When the people go away, the place changes.

When I went back to the campus a couple of years ago, I could hardly spot anybody I knew. That's barring a couple of fellow hostellers who have walked over to the dark side like us and become teachers. Just joking. One of them is a Kaveri hostel warden and lives in the same quarter from which we used to steal water.

Do you remember the bookstore in Kamal Complex? Marx and Marcuse still find a place in the shelves. But I also spotted books like *Devotional Unity with Krishna* and *Sex and Sensuality*. And I saw more Archies greetings card than ever before. Clearly, there's a new demand and supply at work. I am told some students order pizza for dinner nowadays. Materialism seems to have made major inroads in JNU and it is certainly not the dialectical kind.

The political players, too, have changed. The Free Thinkers are gone with the wind. The SFI is still there but the ABVP and AISA, a new radical Left student outfit, have found their feet in the campus.

JNU is in the middle of a major physical make-over too. New hostels have come up. And they are still building more. At this rate, they will soon run out of rivers to name the hostels.

Forgive me, if I sound sarcastic or critical. Nostalgia is an incurable disease. I think we should resist the temptation to look at our days as better than these. The truth is we are all conditioned by the times we live in. These are different times. How can students today be the same as us? Remember how our seniors used to tell us in our first year that JNU changed completely after the 1983 student movement in the campus?

Anyway, nice to reconnect with you. Why don't you come over (with Dori, of course) and stay with us in the coming winter? I will just rephrase what you wrote: remember you always have a home in Jagdalpur.

Affectionately,

Anirban

PS: I miss JNU. And you.